"STOP OR I'LL SHOOT!"

The pair weren't fast and they were already winded. One of them turned and began firing. Longarm stopped, coolly took aim and drilled the man twice in the center of his chest. The remaining assassin ducked into an alley and Longarm went after him. The light was poor, the stench of garbage very strong. Longarm saw the man burst into sunlight at the end of the alley.

"I'm a federal marshal. Stop or I'll shoot!" he ordered.

But the assassin kept running. Longarm tripped over a trash can in the darkness and went sprawling. By the time he managed to get to his feet, his quarry had rounded the corner of another building and vanished. Longarm looked back and forth in two directions, but the man was gone.

"Damn!"

TABOR EVANS

LONGARM AND THE HATCHET WOMAN

JOVE BOOKS, NEW YORK

LONGARM AND THE HATCHET WOMAN

A Jove Book / published by arrangement with
the author

PRINTING HISTORY
Jove edition / September 1998

The Penguin Putnam Inc. World Wide Web site address is
http://www.penguinputnam.com

ISBN: 0-515-12356-0

A JOVE BOOK®
Jove Books are published by The Berkley Publishing Group,
a member of Penguin Putnam Inc.,
200 Madison Avenue, New York, New York 10016.
JOVE and the "J" design are trademarks belonging to
Jove Publications, Inc.

PRINTED IN THE UNITED STATES OF AMERICA

10 9 8 7 6 5 4 3 2 1

Chapter 1

"Look out for trouble in there!" a deputy marshal shouted as Longarm passed through the outer office of the Federal Building. "Marshal Vail's got a big surprise waitin' for ya!"

Before Longarm could form a reply, the entire office erupted in gales of laughter.

"What the hell is so funny?" Longarm asked. When none of his peers answered, he said, "Well, gents, at least I'm not ridin' a damned desk all the time like most of you jackasses."

His comment brought more laughter as he knocked on Billy's closed office door.

"Come in!"

Longarm entered and shut the door behind him, noting that Billy had very important company, including their latest executive director, a political hack who had somehow wangled his appointment by twisting some federal bureaucrat's arm.

Billy practically jumped out of his own desk chair to pump Longarm's hand. "Good to see you, Custis! You know our executive director, Mr. Steven Fenwick."

"Sure do," Longarm said, taking the politician's limp hand and trying not to squeeze it too hard.

Fenwick was short and plump with perfect teeth and manicured hands. He wore white silk shirts and black silk ties, and he always reminded Longarm of a pudgy penguin parading about with self-importance.

Fenwick managed a weak and condescending smile, then continued with the rest of the introductions. "Marshal Long, this is Senator Hal Murray and Assemblyman Larry Turpen."

Longarm shook their hands, and then he turned his attention to the only person in the office who really attracted his interest. She was a pretty woman in her early twenties doing her double damnedest to look unattractive. She wore what was probably an expensive dress, but it reminded Longarm of a uniform. Her hair was pulled back tightly into a bun and she shunned all jewelry—no rings on her fingers or even a pretty ribbon or pin on her collar. Her face was heart-shaped, her eyebrows thick and unplucked. There was an absence of lipstick or rouge, both of which would have vastly improved the woman's appearance and given her some color.

"And this," Fenwick said, "is Miss Katherine Howe."

Longarm bowed slightly, for he had been raised in the South where all men were expected to act like gentlemen. "It's my pleasure to meet you, Miss Howe."

She didn't offer him so much as a smile, nor did she bother to rise from her seat and take his outstretched hand. Instead, Katherine Howe nodded her pointy chin and stared at Longarm as if he were a bug . . . or worse.

Longarm's smile soured and he turned his attention back to Fenwick, who would no doubt explain the purpose of this unusual meeting.

"Miss Howe," the executive director was saying, "is a very close friend of President Rutherford Hayes and his family."

"Oh." Longarm could think of nothing more to say.

"Miss Howe is also quite an accomplished writer and journalist."

"Congratulations," Longarm added without enthusiasm, wondering what in the hell he was supposed to do given this lofty introduction. He glanced at Billy, his frown deepening as he shifted his weight and tried to guess what was coming next. At six-four, Longarm towered over everyone else in the room, and although he was the lowest on the totem pole in terms of importance, his physical presence was dominating.

After a long and uncomfortable silence, Billy cleared his throat and said, "Mr. Fenwick, sir, I haven't had time to exactly discuss the purpose of this meeting with Deputy Marshal Long."

The executive director's eyebrows lifted as if in astonishment. "You mean to say that Marshal Long has no idea *why* we are all gathered here?"

"That's right," Billy replied, beginning to perspire even though his office was cool. "You see, Custis just returned from Montana where—"

"Never mind all that," Senator Murray snapped with annoyance. "Why don't we just get down to brass tacks and find out if this is the right man for the job."

"I'll second that," Assemblyman Turpen added. "Let's not waste any more of our valuable time."

"What job?" Longarm asked suspiciously.

"Why don't we all have a seat," Billy suggested, mopping his brow with a handkerchief. "Custis, I apologize for not finding the time to bring you up to date on what this meeting is about, but. . . ."

"Could we just get on with it?" Miss Howe said in a tone colder than ice. "I also have important things to do. And besides that, I am beginning to suspect that Marshal Long is the wrong man for this assignment. I am an excellent judge of people and I have the feeling that he lacks the . . . the necessary qualifications."

"Now wait a minute, Miss Howe," Billy argued, "Custis is my number-one man!"

"What's the job?" Longarm demanded, feeling his blood pressure starting to escalate.

"Mr. Vail," Fenwick said, "tell your 'number-one man' what you should have told him before this meeting."

"All right," Billy said, turning to Longarm. "We have something of an *unusual* situation here, Custis. A situation that calls for a man of your considerable judgment and great experience. It is a situation that will demand the very best that. . . ."

"Cut the bullshit!" Longarm growled, finally losing his temper. "What is the job?"

Billy took a deep breath. "Custis, have you ever heard of Miss Gertrude Belcher?"

"Sure, she's that old gal that's been raisin' hell back on the East Coast about drinkin'."

"Old gal!" Miss Howe shouted, bouncing up from her chair and finally showing some color in her pale cheeks. "Marshal, how *dare* you refer to Miss Belcher that way! In addition to fighting to outlaw the poison of liquor, Miss Belcher is also a champion of women's suffrage! She has more grit and gumption than you will ever have, and her name will be remembered for generations long after your worthless name is forgotten!"

Longarm was impressed by the outburst. He loved a spunky woman and he had began to think that Miss Howe was a wallflower, so this was definitely an improvement. But on the other hand, he felt that he was being attacked unfairly and that Miss Howe needed to understand his true feelings.

"Miss," Longarm replied with a shrug of his broad shoulders, "I don't give a tinker's damn if my name is remembered or not. Fact is, I'd prefer to be put to my final rest with as little gossip and fanfare as possible. And I sure didn't mean anything disrespectful toward Miss Belcher. Why, from what I have heard and read about the old gal, she's a first-rate rabble rouser. I admire that in a man *or* a woman."

"I have heard more than enough!" Miss Howe said angrily as she left her chair and marched to the door. "That . . . that man personifies the kind of individual that Miss Belcher and I *loathe*! Gentlemen, Marshal Long will not do for this assignment under any circumstances!"

And with that, Katherine Howe slammed the door

with a loud bang that put them all on the edges of their seats.

"Nice going, Custis," Billy said cryptically. "You sure know how to put your foot in your mouth."

"You're a disgrace to my entire operation!" Fenwick exploded, glaring at Custis. "Billy, I'll want a private meeting with you right away!"

The two politicians also glared at Longarm as if he were a criminal . . . or an imbecile. Their looks were so withering that Longarm got mad. "Would someone tell me what in the hell I said wrong and what this meeting was supposed to be about?"

"Sure," Billy said, looking as if he'd just lost his best friend. "Miss Gertrude Belcher—who is also a dear friend of our President—is coming West to campaign for prohibition and a woman's right to vote."

"What in blazes has that got to do with me?" Longarm asked.

"Nothing anymore," Senator Murray said.

"Now wait a minute," Billy declared, raising his hand.

"Custis, what I should have told you before this meeting is that Gertrude Belcher, one of the country's most outspoken but respected women's suffragists, has already received numerous death threats from the West. The reason we are all gathered here is that I was asked to assign my best man to protect Miss Belcher's life on her tour of the Western states and territories."

"You wanted me to nursemaid 'Big Hatchet' Belcher!"

"Please don't use that nickname!" Billy wailed.

"Well, that's what everyone calls her," Longarm answered. "She earned that name, if I remember correctly, because she has been known to enter saloons and use a big hatchet to bust up liquor bottles and casks."

"Marshal," the senator interjected, "Miss Belcher has been known to do that, but not lately."

"I'll guarantee you one thing," Longarm told the politician. "If she tries that out in this part of the country, someone is going to take that hatchet out of her hands and bury it in her skull. Gertrude won't get away with that kind of behavior in a *Western* saloon."

"That's no longer your concern," Fenwick hissed. "It's obvious that you are not man enough to protect the lady."

Longarm would have flattened their executive director if it hadn't been for his friend Billy, who might also suffer the consequences. "Fine! I wouldn't have accepted the job anyway. I have no use for anyone—man or woman—who tries to tell others to stop drinking as they please."

When Longarm reached the door, he turned back to face the room. "You fellas better understand one thing. You may be important, but you sure don't have the right to criticize me, because I've always done my job and upheld the law. I've been shot, stabbed, poisoned, and ambushed over the years tracking down outlaws, and I'm damned proud of my record. Way too proud to turn nursemaid to some female who thinks that she ought to put Western saloons out of business simply because they don't happen to fit her idea of morality."

"You're fired!" Steven Fenwick shouted. "Turn in your badge!"

Longarm reached under his coat and unpinned his

badge. He studied the symbol of what he had stood for all these past years, and thought about the poor pay and hard life following the outlaw trail. He remembered all the times he'd almost been killed trying to arrest some hardcase instead of put him out of his misery. And remembering all that, he tossed his badge on the floor and turned on his heel.

"Where are you going!" Billy shouted.

"Maybe to join the Pinkertons! Or to punch cows or get rich prospecting for gold."

"Longarm, be reasonable! You ain't cowboyed in years! And you don't know a thing about mining!"

"I'm still young enough to learn," Longarm shouted as he stomped across the outer office ignoring the stares of everyone in the room.

"Good riddance," Fenwick grunted.

Billy Vail took a deep breath, then reached into his pocket and removed his own badge. "I'm quitting as well," he said without anger or emotion. "And Mr. Fenwick, you can consider my resignation as being effective right now."

"Now wait a minute!" Fenwick objected, suddenly changing his tune. "You're the most experienced senior officer on staff. Marshal Vail, I require your expertise!"

"And I need my best deputy marshal," Billy replied, glaring at the man. "Mr. Fenwick, there simply isn't anyone else that I'd trust for such an important job. Marshal Custis Long, better known as Longarm, is the only man alive that can keep Gertrude Belcher from getting her head blown off out here. But you've just fired him."

"Well . . . well wait a minute," the executive director said, suddenly looking very worried. "Perhaps this whole thing has been botched from the very beginning. Perhaps we've all been a little bit hasty in our criticism of Marshal Long. I mean, if he is all that special."

"He's the best," Billy said. "No one comes close. He's smart, tough, brave, and savvy. Longarm can smell trouble before it arrives and take the proper steps to handle it under the most desperate circumstances."

"Aren't you gilding the lily just a bit?" Assemblyman Turpen asked. "Sure, he's a big tough-looking fella. That much was apparent the moment he walked into this office. But dammit, he's just a man, and a very insensitive one from what I've seen of him."

"He's not insensitive," Billy declared. "Oh, Custis might be a bit rough around the edges, but he's had to be in order to do his job. What did you expect?"

"You can't talk to me like that!"

"I *am* talking to you like that," Billy said. "But personalities aside, Custis Long is exactly the kind of man that can earn the respect of some fanatic or woman-hater who might try to kill or maim Miss Belcher."

Billy took a deep breath, and his eyes bored into all three of the men who surrounded him. "Gentlemen, Custis is *exactly* the kind of deputy that we need if we really want to protect that woman and avoid the extreme displeasure of our United States President."

"All right," Fenwick conceded. "Get Marshal Long back in here and tell him that he is rehired."

"I don't think that it will be that easy," Billy told his boss. "Longarm is a proud man."

"We're *all* proud men," Senator Murray said, "but sometimes everyone has to eat a little humble pie."

"That's right," Billy told them, "and that time is now."

"What do you mean?" Fenwick asked.

"I mean that you are going to have to offer Marshal Long an apology."

"Never!"

"Then good luck," Billy said, tossing his badge on his desk and reaching for his coat.

"All right!" Senator Murray cried with exasperation. "We ruffled the marshal's feathers. So you get him back here and Fenwick will smooth things over."

"But what about Miss Howe?" Fenwick asked. "She isn't going to accept that man."

"We'll take care of Miss Howe," the senator assured him. "And you will mend your fences with Marshal Long. Is that clearly understood?"

Fenwick understood. He had been given his position by politicians, and there was little doubt in his mind that they could just as easily remove him from office.

"Consider it done," he managed to say.

"Good!" Senator Murray answered as he and Assemblyman Turpen left the office.

"Can you get Longarm to reconsider?" Fenwick asked, looking devastated.

"I don't know" said Billy. "I'm not sure that I want to put him in that position."

"What about *my* position! Don't you realize what this might mean in terms of my career? I could be removed from office if Big Hatchet Belcher is beaten senseless or murdered! This could ruin me!"

"I want a raise in pay," Billy said. "And I want it effective right now."

''How much of a raise?''

''Fifty dollars a month.''

''That's ridiculous!'' Fenwick cried.

''Then I'll write out my resignation today, and I might as well write up Longarm's as well because he won't bother.''

''All right! Fifty-dollars-a-month raise.''

''And fifty for Longarm as a bonus while he's on this Belcher job.''

''That's out of the question! That would mean he would be making—''

''About what he finally deserves. Mr. Fenwick, let's be honest with each other. This will be the worst assignment that any of us could possibly imagine. I've read about Gertrude Belcher and the woman is abrasive and fearless. She won't cooperate with the authorities, and she's even been known to threaten them when they try to protect her. I can't imagine what a nightmare protecting such a person would be like. We saw what a cold fish Miss Howe was, and she's probably a ray of sunshine compared to Big Hatchet.''

''Yeah,'' Fenwick admitted. ''You're probably right. How long is Miss Belcher supposed to be traveling in the West?''

''Almost a month,'' Billy replied. ''She's starting her campaign against liquor and for a woman's right to vote right here in Denver, and then she's going to board the train and go up to Cheyenne.''

''Oh, gawd,'' Fenwick moaned. ''If someone don't kill her here, they'll do it for sure in Wyoming.''

''Yeah,'' Billy agreed. ''And that's why I'm thinking that I had better go along to help Custis.''

"You mean go out in the field and risk your own neck?"

"That's right."

"I can't afford to allow you to do that! I . . . I haven't any idea how to run this operation. You know that."

"Well," Billy said with a shrug of his shoulders, "you'd better start learning fast because even Longarm won't be able to handle this assignment alone. He'll need someone to back him up."

"Then assign him your second-best deputy marshal!"

"Nope," Billy said. "I couldn't live with that. I have to help him out myself, and we had both better be paid for taking on this hellish job."

Fenwick was beaten. "Just . . . just do what you think is best and keep that damned suffragist alive until we can send her back East where she belongs."

"We'll do our very best," Billy promised, "providing, that is, I can persuade Longarm to reconsider."

"Tell him whatever you must but make sure he does."

"He'll expect a personal apology from you, Mr. Fenwick."

"Fine! I'll kiss his hand, if that's what must be done. But go after him right now and bring him back. We've some fences to mend and we had better start doing it right now."

"I couldn't agree more."

"When is Gertrude Belcher supposed to arrive?" Fenwick asked with a forlorn expression.

"Tomorrow afternoon."

"Shit!"

"My sentiments exactly," Billy said, pinning his

badge back on his chest and grabbing his hat. "We'll be back in a few hours."

"Good luck," Fenwick said, looking very depressed.

"Yeah," Billy said as he went to find Longarm. "We'll all need it before Miss Belcher is through with her tour."

"What if Marshal Long refuses to reconsider?"

"I don't know," Billy said, heaving a deep sigh as he set out to find Longarm. "I honestly don't know."

Chapter 2

After leaving the U.S. Marshal's office and the Federal Building on Colfax Avenue, Longarm headed for his rooming house on Cherry Creek. Up ahead, the golden dome of the Colorado State Capitol Building gleamed in the afternoon sunshine, and the summer air was sweet with the perfume of flowers. It was May, one of the best times of the year in this part of the country, and Longarm was feeling unexpectedly optimistic considering that he had just quit his job and hadn't any idea what he would do next for a living.

"Maybe I *will* contact the Pinkertons," he muttered to himself as he strode down the avenue, lost in his own thoughts and still not quite ready to believe that he had resigned from a career for which he was perfectly suited. "But then again, maybe I've pushed my luck too far already and ought to find a little easier line of work."

But Longarm immediately rejected that idea because, to his way of thinking, "easy work" meant "boring work." Sure. He could get a job selling firearms or stocking goods in a mercantile. Or perhaps learning to become a gunsmith or a saddle maker. And for a time, it might prove both satisfying as well as interesting. But Longarm knew that, after a year or two, he'd be completely bored and ready to get back into something more . . . risky. Yeah, risky and dangerous. And while it might be foolish, there was no sense in trying to deny that being a law officer was something that he did well and had always considered to be both important and more than a bit challenging.

"I suppose that I could also find a little frontier town and get myself hired on as a local marshal," he said to himself. "Or maybe I could become a railroad detective or even a bounty hunter."

Longarm had been offered plenty of jobs bringing in criminals for a bounty. But he'd always refused because that was a dirty line of work in which it usually didn't matter whether you brought your man in dead or alive. In fact, most bounty hunters preferred to ambush their quarry and deliver a fugitive draped over a packsaddle. It was simpler and safer to do the job that way and the money was usually the same, regardless of the condition of the man you brought in for the bounty.

Bounty hunting went against Longarm's grain, and he wasn't sure if he would enjoy being a railroad detective. Those gents mostly rode the rails or a desk, and lacked the civil authority to really pursue anyone who had robbed or tried to sabotage their employers.

Longarm scowled, realizing that Billy had been correct. He hadn't worked with cows in years, and he'd make a terrible prospector. Oh, hell, the truth of the matter was that he'd just quit the job for which he was most perfectly suited.

"Custis!"

Longarm snapped out of his ruminations and saw Milly Ralston, a woman who had a questionable reputation but unquestioned beauty. Milly had worked at a number of saloons and shops in the neighborhood and Longarm had flirted with her, but they'd never quite got past that stage.

"Hi, Milly. What's going on?"

"I just lost my job working at Betty's Dress Shop," Milly told him. "They wanted me to wear more conservative clothes and cater to all the wealthy old ladies. But I couldn't do that. I mean, a woman has to be true to herself, doesn't she?"

"You bet," Longarm answered. "I like the way you dress and I'd hate to see you decked out in frumpy, colorless dresses just to please someone else."

Milly smiled. She was short, just over five feet tall, but every inch of it was perfectly proportioned. Milly had large breasts and a narrow waist that flared into almost girlish hips. She was not a raving beauty, but desirable in a pixie-like way that Longarm found more than a trifle attractive. The woman had beautiful brown eyes and wavy hair that fell softly to her shoulders. Milly looked like a schoolgirl, but Longarm knew she was at least twenty-five.

"Custis, what are you doing just walking around today?" Milly asked.

"As a matter of fact, I've also just quit my job and am currently footloose and fancy-free."

"You mean that you're no longer a United States marshal?"

"Correct," Longarm said. "As of about one hour ago, I'm just another regular citizen."

"I thought you liked your work."

"I did," Longarm replied, "but there's times when a man has to stand up for what he believes in."

"A woman too."

"Sure," Longarm agreed. "Everyone has to."

"So what happened?"

Without great elaboration, he told Milly about Gertrude Belcher and the meeting that had taken place in Billy Vail's office. He ended by saying, "Maybe if I'd have been given some warning, things might have turned out differently."

"You mean you'd have agreed to protect Big Hatchet Belcher?"

"So you've heard of her."

"Heck, yes! Who hasn't? That woman must be a holy terror. I understand she has destroyed more than a dozen saloons."

"I wouldn't know about that," Longarm replied, "but I suppose it could be true. Why would a woman do such a thing?"

"You'd have to ask her," Milly said. "Personally, I enjoy getting drunk. Not every day or anything like that, but at least a couple of times a month."

"That's about right," Longarm agreed. "What do you think about women voting?"

"I like the idea. They already gave us the right up in

the Wyoming Territory a few years back. It was the first United States territory or state to do what should have happened everywhere a long time ago,'' Milly said.

''I didn't know that.''

''There's a woman in Wyoming named Esther Morris who had a lot to do with it,'' Milly told him. ''She was appointed a justice of the peace, and I think that made her the first woman judge in the whole wide world.''

''Well I'll be jingoed! Miss Belcher is going up to Cheyenne and I guess she'll want to meet Esther.''

''Probably,'' Milly agreed. ''But I suspect Belcher is more interested in prohibition than women's suffrage. Anyway, it would have been a tough job keeping her alive out in this country.''

''That's for damn sure,'' Longarm agreed. ''How'd you know about Esther and that Wyoming business?''

''I lived in South Pass City a few years ago where Esther Morris lived. I got to know her and always looked up to her.''

''I see.'' Longarm scratched his jaw. ''You know, it seems kind of amazin' to me that I should run into you now just after we both quit our jobs out of principle.''

''Yes, it does. What are you doing for the rest of the day?''

''I was going to buy a bottle of good whiskey and a package of good beef jerky and take 'em up to my room and get drunk.''

Milly giggled. ''So, Custis, you think it's that time of the month?''

''I reckon.''

She stepped up a little closer. ''Maybe you'd like some company. I've got more time on my hands than I do money and I like both whiskey and jerky."

"You do?"

"You bet."

Longarm grinned broadly. "I'll have to fix up some diversion to get you past the owner because we're not supposed to bring women to our rooms."

"I could climb in your window," Milly offered.

"That would work. I'm on the first floor. It would be a whole lot simpler."

"Then let's do it!"

Longarm extended his arm, and Milly slipped her hand through it. They were both smiling when he bought a quart of Old Hound Dog, one of the better brands of local whiskey, and a pound of the best beef jerky in all of Colorado.

"Okay," Longarm said when they reached Cherry Creek and could see his boardinghouse just down on the next block. "My window is the seventh from the northeast corner. I'll pull up the window shade, but you'll have to give me about ten minutes."

"Why so long?"

"The owner is a real talker," Longarm said. "If I can't duck past him while he's napping, there is no way that he will let me go by without jawing about this or that."

"All right," Milly said. "But I don't want to be caught hanging around alone in that back alley. You never know who you'll meet."

"Know what you mean," Longarm said. "The neighborhood is a little rough. I don't worry much, but a woman all by herself sure has to be careful."

"Five minutes," Milly said. "Mind if I take a pull on that bottle before you leave?"

"Help yourself."

Milly took a *long* pull. In fact, she gulped the whiskey down like a man, and it didn't bring tears to her eyes either.

"Ahhh!" she sighed, wiping her cherry-red lips with the back of her hand. "That *is* good stuff. We're going to have a real good time this afternoon, Custis. I always thought we should get together, but I never expected it would take us both quitting jobs to find the opportunity."

"Me neither."

They parted then and Longarm hurried off, praying that Mr. Beesley wouldn't be downstairs in the parlor and wanting to talk. But dammit, he was.

"How you doin', Longarm!" the heavyset old boardinghouse owner shouted. "What in the devil are you doin' back here at this early hour?"

"Long story."

Beesley looked pleased. "I got all the time in the world. What's that in the package? Whiskey?"

Longarm wasn't in the habit of lying, but he made this an exception because if Mr. Beesley got a taste of Old Hound Dog, he would never stop yapping. "Nope. Just some cheap beef jerky."

"Would you mind givin' me a piece? I missed my last meal and my guts are growling."

Carefully, Longarm extracted the jerky, managing to do so without Mr. Beesley seeing the bottle.

"Good jerky!" the rooming house owner exclaimed, enthusiastically smacking his lips. "So now tell me why you are here in the middle of the day when there are so many murderin' sonsabitches on the loose in Denver and everywhere else you can go these days?"

"Well," Longarm hedged, "I'd like tell you all about it, but I'm feeling a bit sickly in the stomach and I might start pitchin' my breakfast all over your floor and makin' a hell of a mess."

"Well, then you had better hurry off to your room!" Beesley said, his smile dying. "I sure wouldn't want to have to clean up any such stinkin' mess!"

"I didn't think so," Longarm told the old man as he hurried on down the hall to his room.

Once inside, he locked the door and then went over to his window and pulled up the shade. "Oh, no," he swore, seeing Milly being accosted by a trio of scruffy ruffians.

Longarm shoved up his window a few inches and yelled, "Get away from her!"

But the men weren't afraid, and they were having fun with Milly. They'd backed her up against a wooden fence and were pawing at her. Longarm tried to push his window up further, but the damned thing was stuck.

"Help!" Milly cried, trying to break free and run to his window. "Custis!"

Longarm was big and he was powerful, but the window was wedged tight and wouldn't slide up high enough for him to climb through. There being no time to lose, he drew his gun and smashed the window to pieces, then did his best to get through without tearing himself up too badly.

"I said to leave her alone!" Longarm shouted as he

advanced on the three ruffians with his gun firmly clenched in his fist.

When the trio saw the gun and how big and strong Longarm was, they turned tail and ran like coyotes.

"You all right?" Longarm asked.

Milly was upset and crying, but she managed to nod her head, saying, "I told you I was afraid of alleys."

"Yeah, I know. And I'm sorry. I was only gone a few minutes, but that's all the time it takes for that sort of vermin to smell out something clean and pretty like you."

She sniffled and dried her eyes with her sleeve. "Do you really think I'm pretty?"

"You're beautiful," he said, taking her in his arms and leading her over to his broken window. "Let me clean this up a little and help you inside."

"Thank you."

Longarm took a few minutes to carefully break all the sharp and protruding pieces of glass from his window. Then he removed his coat and laid it across the windowsill so Milly could climb inside without getting cut by slivers of broken glass.

He pulled the curtain closed and reached for the bottle. "Here," he said, "this will calm your nerves."

Milly's nerves seemed to need a lot of calming, for she drank a good bit of the whiskey. Longarm didn't mind. He could always buy more.

"Feeling better?" he asked when she'd composed herself and given him a reassuring burp.

"A lot better. You got there just in the nick of time."

"Yeah, I expect so."

Milly lifted up on her toes, and still couldn't get high

enough to reach around his neck, so Longarm bent over and they kissed. Her kiss was warm and wet, and he was enjoying it when Milly's little hands unbuttoned his trousers and found his manhood.

"You don't waste any time, do you," he said, leading her over to his bed.

"We've wasted enough time already," Milly answered, stepping back and reaching for the whiskey bottle again.

"Easy on that stuff or you won't enjoy what I have to offer," he warned as he began to remove his gunbelt and then his shirt.

"No chance of that," Milly responded as she took another drink and then quickly began to undress.

When Longarm saw what a perfect little body Milly had, he was immediately aroused. Seeing his manhood stiffen, Milly giggled and then dropped to her knees before him. She took his manhood in her mouth and sucked on it like a little girl on a big lollipop.

"Mmmmmm," she moaned. "Tastes good."

Longarm sighed and closed his eyes. His hips rocked gently back and forth, and he was careful not to start thrusting. As small as this woman was, he could do some serious damage, and he sure didn't want that to happen.

After a while, though, Longarm couldn't stop his hips from thrusting as sweet agony coursed through his groin and made his balls swell up like overly ripe green apples.

"Milly," he groaned, "I think we had better get to my bed or I'm going to pop."

Milly jumped up and pounced on the bed. She spread

her small, shapely legs wide and reached up for him, saying, "Come and get it, Big Boy!"

Longarm did exactly that. Already feverish with desire, he wasted no time in foreplay, but plunged right into Milly, sinking his swollen root in all the way.

"Oh," she gasped. "It feels like I'm being mounted by a horse!"

"You complainin'?"

"No! Come on and show me what you can do, Custis."

Longarm began slowly enough. He started to rotate his hips, and then, every few minutes, to pull his big root out so that its head rubbed up and down on the lips of her honeypot. This drove Milly half crazy with desire, and very quickly she was begging for him to go back deep inside and to pump harder.

Longarm was more than ready to oblige. He sank his root in all the way, and Milly began to thrash and wave her little legs like wings, clutching at his butt cheeks until he finally lost control and began pumping her full of his hot seed.

Milly clung to him with all her limbs, and he could feel her tight little body pumping the last drops of his seed as if each one were the most precious thing in the world. Longarm let her do that as long as she wanted, and then he rolled aside and took her into his arms.

"You were magnificent," she whispered. "Like a great big stallion."

"I'll do it slower next time," he promised. "It'll be slower and even better for the both of us."

"I can't imagine how it could be, but I can hardly wait. How long?"

"Give me an hour and some whiskey and jerky and I'll be a new man before you know it."

"Okay."

For the next hour, Longarm and Milly lay in his bed watching his curtain dance in the breeze while they sipped whiskey and chewed beef jerky and just generally had a fine and happy old time. And then, just when Longarm was starting to get re-aroused, he heard a loud knock on his door.

"Go away, Mr. Beesley, I'm sick and trying to sleep!"

"It's Billy Vail, dammit, and you're not sick and it's way too early to sleep. Open the door, Custis."

"Go away!"

"I *got* to talk to you!"

"We got nothing left to say!"

"I handed in my badge too!" Billy shouted. "Custis, I quit my job right after you did!"

Longarm groaned. "Billy, you got a wife and kids! Why'd you do a fool thing like that?"

"Well, then I changed my mind and pinned the badge back on again."

Longarm was relieved. "Good! Now go away."

"I swear that I'm going to take the assignment of protecting Gertrude Belcher if you won't."

Longarm sat up. "You been out of the field too long, Billy! It's too dangerous."

"I have no choice because no else will do it."

"You'll get yourself killed!" Longarm declared.

"Probably. But not if you agree to pin your badge on again and help me."

"No!"

"I wangled you a fifty-dollar bonus."

"Fifty dollars?" Longarm asked, struggling to escape Milly's grasp. "How'd you do that?"

"Fenwick and the others are desperate. They know they were out of line. Fenwick is even willing to offer you an apology if you'll join me in taking this assignment."

"He will?"

"That's right. And fifty dollars is nothing for you to sneeze at."

Billy was right. Even more important, Longarm knew that Billy would get killed or hurt without protection. Longarm couldn't live with that. He knew and liked Billy's wife and children, and he'd never be able to face them if he didn't agree to this arrangement.

"All right," he said. "But go away and I'll show up in the morning."

"You already got a bottle and a woman in there, don't you."

It wasn't a question, and Longarm wasn't about to deny the fact. "Tomorrow morning, Billy! And get some sleep because you're going to need it helping me to nursemaid Big Hatchet Belcher!"

"I'll give you the same advice, you big bastard!"

Longarm actually laughed as Milly dragged him back onto the bed. She was small, but she was mighty, and there was still a lot of living and loving to do before tomorrow.

Chapter 3

"For crying out loud," Billy growled, "you look like you've been dragged sideways through a knothole! What kind of a woman did you hook yourself up with last night?"

"She was a real spitfire," Longarm conceded, knuckling his bloodshot eyes.

"And you smell like a whiskey barrel."

Longarm wasn't a sensitive man, but he was in no mood for insults this morning. Besides, Billy looked a little ragged himself, and Longarm supposed that his wife and children had not been too thrilled with the idea of him going out in the field after so many years of riding a federal desk chair.

"Look, Billy, why don't you give me the sorry details of this Gertrude Belcher job and then let's just keep away from each other until we are feeling civil."

"I wish we could," Billy replied. "But the truth of the matter is that we have to start preparations right now. Miss Belcher and her entourage are arriving here in Denver sometime early this afternoon, and we need to be ready to greet and protect them."

"How many women is she bringing along on this damned fiasco in addition to that icicle woman."

"You mean Miss Howe?"

"That's right. You don't suppose that they're all going to be that unfriendly, do you, Billy?"

"I sure as hell hope not." Billy shook his head with resignation. "I can tell you right now that I'm no happier than you are about this assignment. We are going to be facing a lot of trials and tribulations for the next month."

"Maybe," Longarm said with a note of hopefulness in his voice, "maybe Miss Belcher and her bunch will see how unpopular their views are in the West and quit the tour early."

"Don't count on it. You'll be surprised how many women are up in arms about not being able to vote except for a few territories and states. And as for liquor, well, I got an earful last night from my wife. As far as she is concerned, more power to the prohibitionists."

"Is that right?" Longarm said with surprise. "I didn't realize that you'd been hittin' the jug that hard, Billy."

"Oh, shut up. I haven't been, but a lot of husbands have been doing too much drinking for a long time. Why, my wife insisted on telling me one story after another about how many of her friends have drunken or abusive husbands. I tell you, some of her stories were downright pathetic."

"Don't quit on me," Longarm warned. "It's going to be hard enough to stand together as men on this tour without you going soft and agreeing with Big Hatchet."

"You just *gotta* stop referring to her by that nickname," Billy pleaded. "If you don't, this whole thing is likely to explode in our faces like a rotten egg."

"It probably will anyway."

"Yeah, maybe, but I'd like to at least put that off as long as possible."

"Sure," Longarm said, leaning back in a chair and dropping his boot heels on Billy's desk. "You're the boss. How are we going to handle the opposition?"

"First off," Billy said, "we need to find out how many women are going to be accompanying Miss Belcher. Maybe it's only going to be one or two."

"If they're all like Miss Howe, even that many will be bad news."

"I know. But let's be optimistic and say that there will only be a couple of suffragists with Miss Belcher when she leaves town and heads up to Cheyenne."

"Did you ever hear of Esther Morris?" Longarm asked.

"Nope. Is she coming too?"

"No, but she's one of the West's leading suffragists. First woman judge in America. A gal told me that she might be waiting for us in Cheyenne even though Esther still lives way over in South Pass City."

"Let's hope that she stays there. From what little information I've received, Miss Belcher doesn't plan to spend much time in Wyoming. From there, she's taking the train to Salt Lake City and then on to Nevada, where she'll probably visit the Comstock Lode as well as

Carson City. After that, I haven't any idea where she'd be headed. My guess is California or south into Arizona."

"Well," Longarm said, "my money says that Gertrude and her coldhearted witches won't get past Salt Lake City before they pack up their brooms and head back East."

"We'll see. But for the moment, we have to get ready to take care of them right here in Denver."

"Are they planning on having a rally or giving speeches this afternoon?"

"I don't think so. I was told by Assemblyman Turpen that Miss Belcher is entirely unpredictable. By that, I mean she'll decide to wade into a saloon or jump up on a bench and start preaching her message at any time or place and without the least bit of warning."

"This is sounding worse by the minute," Longarm complained. "So what is your suggestion?"

"I was hoping you'd have a few."

"Hell, Billy, I work for *you*, not the other way around! If you want my suggestion, you should just stay right here in this office."

"I can't," Billy said. "I already told Mr. Fenwick that I'd take this on personally. Besides, I'm pretty sure that you can use my help."

"Maybe and maybe not." Longarm frowned. "Will you be packing a side arm and a hideout gun?"

"Of course! You think I've forgotten everything?"

"It's been a lot of years, Billy. A man gets rusty and then he makes a mistake and it costs someone their life."

"You just worry about Miss Belcher and her cronies. I'll take up whatever slack there is."

"Fair enough," Longarm answered with a shrug of his shoulders. "In my opinion, we ought to just let things unfold naturally."

"What does that mean?"

"It means that, if Big Hatchet Belcher is anything like Miss Howe, and I suspect she is much worse, then trying to tell her to be careful or to minimize the risks would be a complete waste of time."

"I agree." Billy frowned. "But we can't just let—"

They were interrupted by a firm knock on the door. "We're busy!" Billy yelled.

"So am I! But we have to talk."

"Aw, shit," Billy groaned. "It's Miss Howe. We'd better hear what she has to say."

"I heard enough yesterday," Longarm replied, "but go ahead and open the damned door."

Billy ran his fingers through his thinning hair before he went and opened his door. "Come on inside, Miss Howe."

Longarm nodded a cold greeting. Katherine Howe had insulted him all she was going to in this lifetime.

The woman wore a different dress, but it was every bit as drab and colorless as the one she'd worn the day before. Again, no makeup or jewelry, and this time Longarm noticed that there were dark circles around her eyes. Well, Longarm thought, it would appear that we all had a long night.

"What can I do for you, Miss Howe?" Billy asked, motioning her to a chair.

"I'll only take a moment of your time, Mr. Vail. I just came to say that I'm grateful that you have personally accepted the responsibility for Miss Belcher's safety. I . . . I think that was very good of you."

"Thank you." Billy brightened a little. "And I'd like to think that perhaps we can start over in terms of getting along together. Custis . . . I mean Marshal Long, really is the finest peace officer on my staff."

Katherine Howe deigned to give Longarm a weak smile. "I am sure that he is," she said, turning back to Billy. "But he just *looks* so rough and disreputable."

"Thanks," Longarm drawled. "Miss, in case you haven't noticed, you're no rose blossom either."

Katherine's eyes sparked with anger. "I tell you what, Deputy Long. I'll keep my opinions to myself and you do the same. Is that a deal?"

"Sure, as long as—"

Billy jumped in before a fight began and said, "Miss Howe, it would be helpful if you could tell us what to expect while Miss Belcher is in Denver."

Katherine turned back to him. "I wish that I could, but Miss Belcher is a very free-spirited woman who acts on impulse. Her impulses are almost always correct."

"I'm sure that they are," Billy said dryly. "However, if I had some idea, we could get a few other officers involved."

Katherine nodded. "I can only offer a guess that Miss Belcher will probably speak right out in front of the Denver Mint on those big stairs."

Billy gulped. "She will?"

"It's only a guess," Katherine repeated. "But I've been with her for three years now and I have gotten to where I can predict the kind of settings that she prefers to use as a forum. The federal mint is just the kind of a pulpit that she likes."

"All right," Billy said. "Will she do it on her way over here or on her way out?"

"Probably on her way in. Miss Belcher has the energy of three women and she has been confined to a train, so she will be anxious to preach her message."

"That's good to know," Billy said. "We'll have extra men posted in front of the Denver Mint, although I'm not sure how large a crowd might be there to listen."

"A crowd always shows up wherever Miss Belcher speaks."

"Do you have any idea when she plans to board the train for Cheyenne?"

"Tomorrow afternoon."

Billy shot a surprised glance at Longarm, then turned back to the woman. "That fast?"

"I expect so," Katherine said. "It all depends on how she is feeling and what kind of response she receives from the crowd this afternoon on those stairs."

"Yes, of course," Billy replied. "If she is well received, she might stay an extra day or two. If not, I expect that Miss Belcher will want an early departure from Denver."

"Exactly the opposite," Katherine said. "The more animosity and adversity she gets, the *longer* she will stay."

"Aw, shit," Longarm muttered.

"I beg your pardon, Marshal!" Katherine huffed.

"Never mind," Longarm said, coming out of his chair. "I'll put together a greeting party for Miss Belcher. Billy, why don't you serve this *woman* some hot tea and crumpets?"

Billy blushed with anger and embarrassment, and

would have exploded if it hadn't been for the young suffragist. Instead, he swallowed his outburst and clenched his jaw, managing a nod of agreement.

Longarm was glad to get away from Katherine Howe. He hadn't liked the woman from the moment he'd set eyes upon her, and he never would. The fact that she felt exactly the same way about him was quite convenient. He went out to the outer office and started rounding up the deputy marshals and telling them to get ready to go to work.

"Miss Belcher is a personal friend of our United States President," he said. "If she is shot, heads will roll in this building, so you gents have more than a small stake in keeping her alive and healthy."

No one was laughing anymore about Miss Belcher because they realized the seriousness of the situation. "Who is meeting her train?" one young deputy asked.

"We are," Longarm said. "We meet the train, then escort her into town. Let's go!"

"Custis, do you know what she looks like?"

"I expect this woman won't be hard to miss," Longarm replied. "Generally, we'll just hang in around her like a loose net and herd her on down to the Federal Building. If she stops on the stairs of the Denver Mint and wants to preach her gospel, then we move in a little closer."

"Who would want to kill her?"

"Damned if I know," Longarm replied. "But you can bet it won't be a woman."

"Oh, yeah?" one of the deputies said as they started for the door. "I don't think we can assume that. What if some gal who works in a saloon and is afraid of losing her job shows up with murder on her mind?''

''Good point,'' Longarm said. ''So we had better watch everyone but kids.''

''Could be some kid whose father owns a saloon . . .''

''Aw shut up,'' Longarm growled. ''Let's just get down there and do the best we can.''

The moment the train pulled to a stop, Gertrude Belcher burst into view. Longarm was taken completely by surprise because the suffragist was gray-haired and barely five feet tall, but her quick, almost military stride gave evidence of great energy and purpose. Belcher was closely followed by a woman who was at least six feet tall and weighed two hundred pounds. That, Longarm realized, would be Belcher's bodyguard, and she looked plenty equal to the task. Longarm wondered if the big woman wore a gun and knew how to use it.

''Miss Belcher!'' Billy shouted, rushing forward to meet the famous woman. ''Welcome to Denver!''

The train was hissing and letting off steam, so Longarm couldn't hear Belcher's reply, but he did see Billy's smile dissolve and then watch him jump backward. A moment later, Billy was trailing the suffragist and heading for downtown.

Longarm signaled for his men to hurry forward and overtake the women. There really wasn't any need for them to make their presence known, but they did need to be in a proper position to shield Gertrude Belcher in case some crazy assassin was waiting up ahead.

As they rushed toward downtown, a crowd began to gather and, for the first time, Longarm realized that this woman really was famous—or infamous—depending on one's personal point of view. And by the time they reached downtown, there must have been three hundred people following along. Some of them, of course, wouldn't have the vaguest idea that this was Big Hatchet Belcher, but would simply be drawn along by curiosity. But most of the crowd definitely knew Gertrude Belcher, and some of the women were even waving placards that had messages like: "DOWN WITH DEMON RUN!" "GIVE WOMEN THE RIGHT TO VOTE!" "LIQUOR IS THE DEVIL'S BREW!"

Longarm had to admit that Miss Belcher knew how to attract attention. She was dressed entirely in black, as if in mourning, and she kept pumping her knotted fists into the blue Colorado sky and repeatedly shouting, "Liberty and temperance! Liberty and temperance!"

The woman was whipping up the crowd.

"We're in for trouble," Longarm told one of the deputies. "The smartest thing to do is to get Belcher inside the Federal Building as soon as possible where we have a much better chance of protecting her."

"Any idea of how to do that?"

"No."

Belcher suddenly bounded up the concrete steps in front of the Denver Mint, just as Katherine Howe had predicted. Raising her arms, she commanded the crowd to be silent.

"My friends," she began in a raw but powerful voice, "too long have the women of America been denied our right to vote. Are we second-class citizens?"

Every woman in the crowd echoed, "No!"

"And what about devil rum! What about America's children who will never know their fathers because they died of alcohol or were killed in a saloon fight or wasted their lives and ran off in shame to die in the gutter!"

"Holy cow," Billy said, pushing over to Longarm. "This woman is going to incite a damned riot!"

"I don't see how you can stop her," Longarm replied, feeling the emotion that was already starting to build. The crowd was growing larger and larger. There were now at least three hundred people, and more were arriving every minute.

"I'll put it to you straight!" Belcher shouted. "If the sober people of this great country would find enough backbone to smash the liquor stills and pour demon rum into the streets instead of down the throats of those it is sure to destroy, then America could be strong and sober again!"

The women and a lot of the men on the street bellowed their support and agreement.

"And," Belcher yelled, "we would have fewer murders! Fathers would not beat and abandon their families! Wars that we have not yet fought will be averted! Man and womankind would at last be unshackled from a terrible affliction and free to pursue harmony and God!"

"Hey, Billy," Longarm said, noticing a familiar face in the crowd, "isn't that your *wife* waving that sign?"

Billy's eyes bulged. "Damned if it isn't! What . . ."

Whatever more Billy was about to say was lost in the sound of gunfire. Longarm saw Gertrude's bodyguard stagger at the impact of a bullet, then struggle to pull a gun out of her dress pocket a moment before she collapsed. There were more gunshots mixed with shrieks of terror. Billy sprinted forward, and then was shot down as the crowd scattered like quail.

Longarm's gun was in his fist, but there was so much chaos and confusion that only a fool would have opened fire. With so many people running and screaming, he was unable to identify the assassin or assassins as he hurried toward Billy, who was struggling to climb back to his feet. Gertrude Belcher was shouting and pointing, and when Longarm followed her gaze, he at last was able to identify two men racing up the street with guns in their fists.

"Get them!" Gertrude Belcher screamed. "Bring those murderers to justice!"

Billy was yelling too, only his voice was too weak to be heard. Longarm knew that his responsibility was to go after the assassins. He leapt over prostrate spectators and knocked more than a few down in his headlong sprint to close the distance between himself and his quarry.

"Stop! You're under arrest!" he shouted at the first intersection when he was only about thirty yards behind. "Stop or I'll shoot!"

The pair wasn't fast and they were already winded. One of them turned and began firing. Longarm stopped, coolly took aim, and drilled the man twice in the center of his chest. The remaining assassin ducked into an alley, and Longarm went after him. The light was poor, the stench of garbage very strong. Longarm saw the man burst into sunlight at the end of the alley.

"I'm a federal marshal. Stop or I'll shoot!" he ordered.

But the assassin kept running. Longarm tripped over a trash can in the darkness and went sprawling. By the time he managed to get to his feet, his quarry had rounded the corner of another building and had vanished. Longarm looked in both directions, but the man was gone.

"Damn!" He cursed and wiped garbage from his suit coat.

Then he holstered his gun, pivoted on his heel, and ran back to the Denver Mint, hoping that Billy Vail and Gertrude Belcher's bodyguard were both still alive.

Chapter 4

When Longarm arrived back at the steps of the Denver Mint, the scene was still one of great confusion. The other deputies had attempted to escort Gertrude Belcher away to the Federal Building for her own protection, but Gertrude had staunchly refused. Her female protector was dead, struck by a bullet in the head. Billy Vail was alive, and had already been rushed to the nearest hospital with a slug buried deep in his shoulder.

"Billy is definitely going to make it," one of the deputy marshals told Longarm. "But if that assassin's bullet had been just two inches lower, he would have ended up just like that big woman. She gave her life for Miss Belcher."

"I know," Longarm said. "I wish I'd have had a chance to at least know her name."

"Did you kill the ones that got her and Billy?"

"I shot one, but the other escaped."

"Did you get a good look at him?"

"Yeah, and his face is vaguely familiar. I'll recognize him when I see him again."

The deputy, whose name was Bob Hinton, expelled a deep breath. "Custis, what should we do now?"

"Let's get the remainder of this crowd cleared out and then get Big Hatchet up to our offices. I've got some hard questions to ask her."

"You'd better go easy," Hinton advised. "She's real upset about that woman dying."

"Well," Longarm said, "I'm *real* upset about Billy getting shot. That woman was just asking for trouble the way she was stirring up the crowd. What did she expect anyway?"

"I'll tell you what she expected," Katherine Howe angrily answered as she came up behind them. "She expected your protection and the right of free speech without being shot to death! And as far as I'm concerned, you were no help at all!"

Longarm started to explode, but Hinton pushed in front of him and said, "Miss Howe, Custis and the rest of us did all that we could to warn you that there could be trouble here."

"We expect protection! Two people shot and the assassins escape without—"

"Custis gunned down one of them," Hinton interrupted. "And he recognized the other. We'll get him too, Miss. He'll stand trial for the murder of that big gal and you can bet that he'll hang."

"I certainly hope so!"

"Help us get Miss Belcher over to the Federal Building before some other madmen show up,'' Longarm snapped. ''We can carry on this conversation inside.''

''Fine!''

Once they were up in the Federal Building, Longarm started to tear into Gertrude Belcher, and he didn't much give a damn about the consequences. A brave woman was dead and Billy was fighting for his life in a nearby hospital. By gawd, it *was* all Gertrude Belcher's fault!

''Miss Belcher,'' Longarm said, ignoring his executive director, ''I think this ought to convince you that a tour of the West is just too damned dangerous. Next time, it could be you or Miss Howe who gets shot to death.''

''Or you,'' the older woman said. ''Is *that* what's really got you worried, Marshal Long?''

''Hell, no! But I'm not about to throw away my life on this foolishness.''

Gertrude raised her eyebrows. She had to crane her head back in order to gaze up into Longarm's eyes. ''You call this foolishness?''

''I do.''

''Then I don't want you around anyway.''

''Fine.''

''You're not getting off that easy,'' Fenwick shouted. ''Marshal Long, you agreed to do this and you will do it *before* you are allowed to resign!''

''Why should I?''

''Because,'' Steven Fenwick said, ''I've just returned from Billy's side at the hospital and he told me to make you keep your word.''

Longarm ground his teeth together. The very last thing in the world he wanted was to try to protect Big

Hatchet Belcher, but if Billy felt that strongly about it, then there was little choice but to agree.

"Miss Belcher, when are we leaving Denver?" Longarm asked.

"Katherine and I will discuss that tonight and let you know tomorrow," the woman replied. "Now, take me to this hospital so I can see that wounded marshal and tell him how grateful I am to him for keeping any more people from being shot."

Longarm managed to nod his head. "All right."

When they got to the hospital, Billy was in worse shape than expected. He was conscious, but very weak, and his doctor took Longarm aside and said, "You can only have a minute or two with Mr. Vail because of the seriousness of his condition."

"Sure," Longarm said tightly.

He didn't like the fact that Gertrude Belcher was also going in to see Billy, but saw no use in complaining. When they entered Billy's room, Longarm was shocked by his friend's lack of color. Billy was ghost-white and his breathing was labored.

"Hey," Longarm said, hurrying over to the marshal's bedside. "You almost bought yourself a one-way ticket to the undertaker's."

"Yeah, I know," Billy whispered. "Miss Belcher?"

"Yes?"

"I'm sure sorry about your friend."

"You did all that was humanly possible, Mr. Vail, and I am in your debt."

Billy closed his eyes for a moment, then opened them and said, "Miss Belcher?"

"Gertrude."

"All right, Gertrude. I . . . I think you ought to call off your tour. It's just too dangerous."

"I can't do that," she answered. "If I did, then Constance's death on those stairs today would be in vain."

"We can't protect you," Billy wheezed. "There's no way to predict when another madman or two might open fire in any one of the states or territories where you plan to speak."

"I know that. But I've come a long way to speak my piece. I'll not be sent back East until I've preached about the evils of demon liquor and the equal and indisputable right of every last American woman to vote."

Billy rolled his eyes toward Longarm and struggled to say, "Custis, you're going to have to do this without me. Will you?"

Longarm just couldn't say no. "Sure."

"Gertrude?" Billy said, looking back to the woman.

"Yes?"

"Custis is the *only* man I'd trust. And don't blame him for what happened today. He wanted to be posted next to you, but I thought . . ."

Billy's voice died, and the doctor pushed between them to say, "No more conversation. He's exhausted and needs a lot of rest."

"Okay," Longarm said. "But you're sure that he will recover all right?"

"Unless he gets pneumonia or some other infection. Those things are unpredictable, but barring that, he should have a complete recovery."

That was all that Longarm need to hear. He turned on his heel and stomped out of the room. Gertrude caught up with him and said, "Where do we meet in the morning?"

"Up at Billy's office, I reckon."

"Is eight o'clock too early for you?"

"Hell, no!"

"Eight o'clock then."

Gertrude stuck out her hand, but Longarm ignored it. Billy Vail was one of his best friends and had it not been for this woman, Billy would still be happy and healthy. As far as Longarm was concerned, it was time to go have a few drinks and try to put this entire day out of his mind.

Maybe, he thought, he would hunt up Milly and the two of them could commiserate about their current misfortunes.

He hadn't found Milly the night before, and so had gone to bed early and after only a few beers. The saloon talk all over Denver was about Big Hatchet Belcher and the shootings. Longarm had kept his silence, but it had rankled him to no end to hear that some of the men drinking in his favorite saloon believed that it was too bad that Belcher hadn't been shot because that would have shut her up once and for all.

"Well, Miss Belcher, what's it to be?" Longarm asked when he arrived at Billy's office the next morning to find the two suffragists visiting with Steven Fenwick. "Have you changed your mind about this speaking tour?"

"Of course not," she replied. "But Katherine and I have agreed that since Wyoming and Utah Territories have already given women the right to vote, we might be better advised to skip Cheyenne and go straight to Reno and the Comstock Lode."

Longarm did not try to hide his relief. This was a smart decision, and he told the woman so, adding, "You can go to Nevada, but I think it would be a waste of your time because the miners out there aren't ever going to stop drinking hard spirits. The life is too hard for them."

"It would be much easier for them if they were sober," Katherine argued with her thick eyebrows knotted in disapproval. "You ought to understand that liquor always makes the trials of life seem worse, not better."

"You have a right to your opinion," Longarm responded, "but I think you'd be much better off to skip the *entire* West and both go back where you came from."

"Marshal Long!" the executive director protested. "That kind of comment will not be tolerated."

"Sorry." Longarm gave them a forced grin and said, "When are we leaving Denver?"

"On today's train," Gertrude replied.

"That suits me down to the ground," Longarm told them. "The sooner we leave the sooner we finish. And now, if you'll excuse me, I'm going to go by the hospital and see Billy, then go pack. I'll meet you ladies at the train station."

"Not *ladies,*" Gertrude Belcher said. "*Women.*"

"Yeah," Longarm said, "that is more appropriate and there *is* a big difference."

When Longarm returned to the hospital, Billy was looking much better, and he tried to give Longarm some advice about what to expect on the tour.

"Save your breath," Longarm told his friend. "I'll stick to the both of them like glue. I'll sleep at the foot of their beds like a big pet hound and—"

"Don't be a smart ass," Billy said. "Just get them through this thing alive and well. If you do that, I'll be in your debt and so will the entire department, especially Mr. Fenwick."

"What more could I ask for?"

"You got a bad attitude."

"I got a bad assignment," Longarm replied. "But mark my words, Billy. I'll get through this and send both of those women back to the East in good health."

Billy managed a smile. "Yeah," he said. "I'm betting on it. And by the way, I want to thank you for getting one of the bastards that shot me yesterday."

"My pleasure." Longarm smiled. "I remembered the name of the one that got away. It was Clyde Johnson."

"That horse trader that we had trouble with last year?"

"The very same," Longarm answered. "I'll tell the boys to keep an eye out for Clyde, but I expect he's on his fastest horse headed for Mexico."

"He'll eventually come back," Billy said. "And when he does, we'll still be here and we'll get him."

"I just hope that I'm around to enjoy watching Clyde hang for shooting that big woman."

"Her name was Miss Constance Hall."

Longarm was ready to leave, and picked up his hat.

"Custis?"

"Yeah?"

"I'm sorry you're getting such a dirty job."

“That’s okay. Actually, I’m starting to find a little respect in my heart for Gertie Belcher.”

“Gertrude.”

“Sure,” Longarm said. “And by the way, have you seen her hatchet yet?”

Billy squeaked out a weak laugh and shook his head.

“Me neither,” Longarm said, “but I’m going to keep an eye out for it. If she goes on one of her famous rampages breaking up bottles and hacking up whiskey barrels, that ought to be quite a sight.”

“Forget the damned hatchet. Just keep her alive.”

“I will,” Longarm said as he headed out the door.

Chapter 5

They were hounded all the way to the train depot the following afternoon by a noisy crowd of reporters and citizens. From what Longarm could tell, most of the people were upset about the shootings, and there were several shoving and shouting matches between Gertrude Belcher's supporters and her loudest detractors.

"I'm glad to be out of here," Longarm said when they were finally seated in a passenger compartment. Katherine looked tired and worried, so he added, "is it like this everywhere you women go?"

"No," Gertrude said, answering for her aide, "but I'll have to admit that we've had more opposition than even I expected since we left St. Louis."

"I don't mean to be a wet blanket, ma'am, but I hope you know that things could get even worse, especially when we reach Nevada. If you want my opinion, the last place you want to visit would be the Comstock Lode."

"Why?" Katherine asked. "Why would it be any worse than, say . . . Denver?"

"The Comstock Lode is about the wildest place in the West," Longarm said, having the feeling that Katherine was also starting to question this speaking tour. "In the first place, about ninety-five percent of the Comstock population are men. Most of them are miners, freighters, cutthroats, and thieves. They don't have time to worry about women having the right to vote. When they do have a little money, the only places they can go to relax are the saloons."

"What a shame."

"Maybe so, but to those hardworking men, a saloon is the next best thing to being home. It's where men meet, drink, talk, and have a few laughs. And sure, sometimes things will get out of hand, but that is expected."

"I've heard that the number of murders on the Comstock Lode is horrendous," Katherine said.

"It's a wild town that never shuts down."

"Is there no law and order there?" she asked.

"Not much. They have a marshal and a few deputies, but Virginia City, Gold Hill, and Silver City have always been either boom or bust and the local politicians are real tightfisted. The truth of the matter is that they can't pay their lawmen enough money to keep them on the job. At least, not good lawmen. You see, the Comstock Miners Union has set wages so high that—"

"How high?" Gertrude asked.

"Three dollars a day."

"It's very dangerous work," Gertrude said. "Marshal, it might help you to understand that my father was a Welsh coal miner who worked most of his life down in the deep mines of the British Isles. He died in a cave-in when he was just twenty-eight years old, and that was about the average length of life of a Welsh coal miner. From what I've heard of the Comstock Lode, the conditions aren't much safer and the depths that they are working in are considerably deeper."

"That's true."

"And it's also true that if the Comstock Miners spend their money on wholesome pursuits, then they'd live longer, happier, and more productive lives."

"They're free men," Longarm argued, "and free men ought to be able to choose how they live."

"Not when how they live is detrimental to society and to themselves," Katherine told him. "And that is why there are laws against many other dangerous drugs."

Longarm snorted. "Liquor isn't a drug."

"Of course it is," Gertrude argued. "And it kills more men, ruins more families, and creates a more devastating toll on society than any other poison. The simple fact of the matter is, Marshal, liquor must be outlawed."

"It will never happen," Longarm stated.

"You're wrong about that," Katherine told him. "There are prohibitionist movements springing up all over the East. And in Kansas, the legislature is considering a state constitutional amendment to outlaw liquor."

"The people will never stand for that," Longarm predicted. "The only territory where liquor might stand a chance of being outlawed is Utah, where most of the folks are Mormon and don't drink anyway."

"Marshal," Gertrude said, "I'm glad that you were asked to come along because, if I can convince you of the evils of liquor and the need for prohibition, then I can convince anyone."

Longarm didn't quite know how to respond to that, so he just nodded his head and turned to look out the window. This journey up to Cheyenne was one of his favorites, and he was sure to see plenty of pronghorn antelope. Fast and elusive, they were one of the few species of game that had managed to survive the onslaught of civilization and the fencing of the American West.

Longarm and the two women stayed overnight in Cheyenne, and left the following morning with very little fanfare on the Union Pacific bound for Sacramento. There were some well-wishers who came to see Big Hatchet, as well as a few drunken hecklers that Longarm sent packing with a stern warning that he would not hesitate to have them arrested.

As they began to roll out of Cheyenne, some wild cowboys came chasing after their railroad car, waving pistols and whiskey bottles. Drinking, hooting, and shouting obscenities that were fortunately drown out by the sound of the train, the cowboys chased the train nearly two miles before their winded horses began to tire. The horsemen fired their pistols into the air, and one was so drunk that he toppled out of his saddle and his horse ran back in the direction of town.

"Doesn't a sight like that sicken you?" Katherine asked.

"Nope. They were just letting off a little steam the same as the locomotive that is pulling this car."

''Oh, no,'' Gertrude said, wagging her head back and forth. ''This train is being productive, while those cowboys were wasting their time and their money on bullets and liquor. They were also endangering their very lives.''

''I very much doubt that,'' Longarm said, trying to hide a smile. ''Heck, most of those fellas were hardly more than kids.''

''All the sadder then,'' Katherine said, folding her arms across her breast. ''The earlier they begin to drink demon liquor, the sooner they will become addicted and their health and sanity begin to fail.''

Longarm gave up. These women were fanatics and there was no point in trying to reason with them. Besides, he needed a drink and them some dinner in the dining car because his stomach was growling. But what would they say when he ordered a whiskey while waiting for his meal? Oh, he thought, the hell with what they're gonna think. Besides, I'll be damned if I'm going to abstain just because of their narrow-mindedness. If they don't like me having a few drinks when I want, then they can either look the other way or leave the room.

Having reached that decision, Longarm stood up in their private compartment and announced, ''Ladies . . . I mean *women,* I'm hungry enough to eat the . . . well, I'm real hungry. The dining car is two doors up ahead and I'm going to have myself a whiskey or two and then maybe even a glass of red wine with a half-raw piece of Wyoming beef.''

''Why are you telling us this?'' Katherine asked, eyebrows knitted with disapproval.

"He's not *telling* us," Gertrudc said, "he's *warning* us. Isn't that right, Marshal?"

"Yes it is, Gertrude. I figure it is better that you know right off that I have no intention of giving up liquor on this tour."

"I appreciate your frankness," the suffragist told him. "And as long as you don't overindulge, and remain sober and capable of carrying on your duties as a law officer, I won't object."

"Fair enough," Longarm replied. "I won't get drunk or in any way embarrass you. And I'm glad that we reached this understanding in private."

"I agree," Gertrude said, looking to Katherine, who didn't appear as if she agreed at all. However, the younger woman was wise enough to keep whatever objections she had to herself.

"Are you coming along to eat with me, or would you prefer to eat at your own table?" Longarm asked.

"We are tired and I think we would rather eat alone," Gertrude decided. "Marshal, will you ask a porter or one of the dining car attendants to please bring us a dinner menu that we can order from our private compartment?"

"Sure," he told them on his way out. "But you know where to find me if you—"

"We will say good night," Gertrude told him, "and see you in the morning. Perhaps we can meet in the dining car for breakfast, or do you also drink liquor at that early hour?"

"No, ma'am," he said with a smile. "I never drink hard liquor before noon. That is, unless I'm hung over."

''I see. Very good. Then let's meet at eight o'clock for breakfast.''

''Sure thing.''

Longarm went up to the dining car, ordered a double whiskey and his dinner, then sat back to watch sundown grace the western Wyoming landscape. It was a pleasant time, and since the dining car was full and the attendants busy, it took nearly an hour to get his steak, which turned out to be excellent. Feeling very relaxed after two whiskeys and a glass of red wine, he ordered coffee and apple pie for dessert, and made sure that someone was going to take care of the two Eastern suffragists, who would probably be famished.

Longarm was feeling much better about his immediate future. Big Hatchet Belcher, or Gertrude, wasn't such a bad old gal after all. She could be reasonable, which was a very pleasant surprise. In fact, Longarm was beginning to suspect that she was far more tolerant than Miss Katherine Howe.

What was the younger woman's problem? Why was she such a fanatic about liquor and so passionate about all women having the right to vote? They had earned it in the Wyoming and Utah territories, and if memory served him correctly, also in Washington Territory just a few years ago. Sooner or later, they'd also have it in Colorado, and then every state and territory in the Union. The thing of it was that they would only hurt themselves by being too forward and vocal. Yes, sir, that could and probably would cause a backlash.

''Marshal!''

Longarm twisted around to see an excited man in a tan suit rush into the dining car. He held a chubby hand tight over one of his eyes and he looked half dazed.

"Marshal," the man wailed, "you'd better get back to help them women!"

Longarm jumped out of his seat so fast that he almost knocked his table flying. "What's wrong?"

"There's a couple of drunks giving those Eastern ladies a real bad time. I tried to help, but one of them punched me in the eye, dammit!"

Longarm didn't need to hear any more, and was instantly racing out of the dining car and on his way to the rescue. He knocked a man over, and then, just before he reached the car where Gertrude and Katherine were staying, he heard a gunshot.

"Oh, no!" he stormed, barreling down the aisle and finally reaching the sleeping coaches.

When he barged into the coach, the light was very poor, but the first thing he saw was a man screaming as if he was about to be slaughtered. Kneeling in the aisle, he clasped his forearm and his coat was soaked with blood. Another man was lying facedown in the aisle twitching.

"What happened!" Longarm shouted as he rushed down the aisle.

"It's all right," Gertrude said, emerging from their compartment.

"It don't look all right to me!"

Gertrude pointed to the man on the floor and ignored the one who was screaming and squeezing his wounded forearm. "That one tried to assuault Katherine. He was drunk and could not be talked into leaving. When he grabbed for Katherine, she pulled a derringer from her purse and shot him."

Longarm's eyes jumped to the younger woman, and that was when he saw the derringer clutched in her fist. He stared at her and then asked, "*Where* exactly did you shoot him?"

"In the . . . groin," Katherine answered. "It was my intention to castrate him with a bullet, and I'd be surprised if I did not. I am a good shot and I fired at point-blank range."

Longarm glanced at the other man. "What about him?"

Gertrude raised a bloody hatchet. "I hope that his arm won't have to be amputated," she said, "but he ignored all my warnings and this was the only weapon I could depend upon."

"Jaysus," Longarm breathed. He spun around and shouted, "Someone see if there's a doctor on this train! If not, bring bandages!"

"I was trained as a nurse," Katherine said. "I'll have a look at them."

"I think you've done plenty already," Longarm snapped. "Why don't you both go back inside and rest for a few minutes while I get these fools some medical attention."

"I'm sorry that this had to happen," Katherine said. "But you weren't here to do your job and they are drunk."

"Yeah," Longarm answered. "Get inside and say no more. I'm in charge now."

"Marshal," Katherine said, bitterness in her voice, "have you noticed how you always arrive just a little late?"

"Don't mind her," Gertrude said. "Katherine is very

upset and we really haven't recovered from losing Constance yesterday."

"That's perfectly understandable," Longarm said, his words belying the fact that he had been stung by Katherine's remark.

Fortunately, there was a doctor on the train and he was able to tend the two assailants. It was not until the following morning that Longarm learned that one of them had suffered a grievous injury in his groin that might render him sterile. As for the hatchet wound, it had caused a great deal of bleeding, but there would be no permanent physical damage.

Longarm held both men under arrest, and he would drop them at the next Wyoming town that had a judge.

"Is it true that the young one shot that fella in the balls?" a passenger asked Longarm the following morning. "And that the other almost had his arm hacked off by Big Hatchet?"

"That's right."

"Marshal," the passenger said with amazement and a healthy dose of respect, "those Eastern women suffragists sure don't need *your* protection."

"I'm beginning to think not," Longarm growled in a tone that left no room for further comment.

Chapter 6

They spent only one uneventful night in Salt Lake City, where the two suffragists were feted by a large contingent of prohibitionists, most of whom were Mormons. Longarm didn't need to worry much about trouble. Then they boarded the westbound train and headed for Nevada. It was there, Longarm knew, that they were most likely to run into the stiffest and most dangerous opposition. Not that he was aware of any specific group that might be ready to create havoc for the two Eastern women, but it was just that Nevada was so wild and untamed. It was a big state and its citizens often settled their differences with their fists, a gun, or a hangman's rope.

Longarm's eyes were closed and he was daydreaming as their train followed the general southwestern path of the Humboldt River. He was remembering a time not too many years ago when he'd chased a train robber named Red Killion out through this high desert wilderness. It had been extremely hot, and had it not been for the foul-tasting water of the Humboldt River, they'd both have died of thirst. As it was, Killion's horse had gone lame, enabling Longarm to overtake and get the drop on the outlaw. Two days later, and still more than a hundred miles from any settlement, they were jumped by Paiutes and . . .

"Excuse me. Marshal Long, would you mind if I joined you for a few minutes? I'd like to talk with you privately."

He opened his eyes to see Katherine standing beside his seat. She looked nervous and upset, which was not all that surprising considering the fact that she had shot and probably castrated a man. Not trusting what kind of business she had in mind to discuss, Longarm nevertheless nodded his head in agreement. "Sure. Sit down, Miss Howe."

"Katherine."

"Sit down, *Katherine*."

She sat, and said nothing for a very long time. Finally, Longarm grew impatient and said, "What is it you wanted to discuss?"

"Oh, nothing all that important. Were you asleep just now?"

"Daydreaming," he confessed. "I was thinking about an outlaw that I once tracked across this desert wilderness."

"I assume you apprehended him."

"Yeah."

"Did he go to trial and hang?"

"No," Longarm told her. "Red Killion wasn't a murderer. He robbed stagecoaches and trains. Probably hit a bank in Winnemucca and walked away with almost ten thousand dollars, but no one knows for certain."

"But he never shot anyone."

"He might have wounded a few, but he wasn't a cold-blooded killer. Red was actually a pretty nice fella except for his penchant for wanting other people's money."

"I see. And I suppose he's now moldering in some federal prison?"

"Nope," Longarm said, "I buried him on that low hill just up yonder with the red rocks breaking out on the top. Didn't bury him very deep because I was in a bad fix and had no shovel. I did the best that I could, though, under some grim and dangerous circumstances."

"Did you kill the man?"

"The Paiutes killed him," Longarm told her. "They were raiding and we just happened to have the misfortune of crossing their path. I have generally found the Paiutes to be reasonable, but this band was no good."

"How . . . ?"

"They set an ambush that caught us by surprise. One of the Paiutes must have had a Sharps buffalo rifle and knew how to use it, because the hole he opened in Red's chest was big enough to put your fist through. Not that anyone would, of course."

Katherine's lips pinched at the corners. "But you were luckier?"

"That's right. They shot my mount right out from under me, but Red's horse ran away and I was able to chase him down after dark and put some miles between myself and those murdering Paiutes. A couple weeks later when things were under control and that band of renegade Indians were raising hell way down south, I rode back up here and buried what was left of Red's body. Wasn't much, though. The hot sun parched everything that the scavengers didn't eat."

Katherine made a face. "You sure have a way with words, Marshal Long. Sort of an understated manner that is quite disgusting."

"You asked me to tell you what happened, remember?" Longarm snapped. "I wouldn't have told you about Red Killion and how he ended up if you hadn't asked."

"Yes," she admitted, "that's true. And that's the hill where you buried the outlaw?"

"It is," he said. "I can tell because of that big old twisted juniper that is poking up through the red rocks."

"Didn't you attempt to find out if this outlaw had any beloved relatives that might have wanted to disinter his earthly remains and give the poor man a Christian burial?"

"Red had lots of relatives, and most of them were far worse than he was. None of 'em ever earned an honest dollar. They were bad to the bone, and I doubt that there's a free-runnin' Killion man under the age of eighty to be found in this territory. At least four of them I know of have met violent ends, and most of the others are in jail or prison."

"You sound as if you think that they had some kind of bad blood."

"I do," Longarm said with conviction. "Every one

of them was sneaky, lazy, and a thief. Like I already told you, Red was probably the best of the lot, but even his own mother wouldn't claim him."

"That's extremely sad," Katherine said. "Is it typical of the Western bad man?"

"I don't know if there is any 'typical' Western outlaw," Longarm answered after giving the question some thought. "A lot of them just turned to crime because they knew that if they didn't find a way out of the hard life they were leading, they'd probably die young. Wherever you find a man that has no reasonable hope of bettering himself, you've got a potential outlaw. Don't matter if it's out here in Nevada or in Boston or New York City. I believe that hope is what keeps us all at least partly honest. It's the universal hope of man that things can and will get better."

"I don't believe that," Katherine said, looking him right in the eye. "There are millions of poor in this world who have little or no hope of prosperity or even enough food to eat for themselves and their families. Why, I'm told that entire countries have populations that live considerably worse than the stupid livestock they tend! And those poor, hopeless people aren't thinking about becoming criminals."

"Maybe they have a religion that promises them a better life next time around or a place in heaven."

"Marshal, are you an atheist?"

"Nope. And religion does give a poor person a fair measure of hope and consolation."

Katherine's eyes sparked with anger and outrage. "There is nothing wrong with that!"

"I couldn't agree with you more," Longarm said, unwilling to become perturbed but tiring of the conversation. "Katherine, if you have something you want to talk about *other* than politics or religion, why, I'm happy to oblige. But if not . . . then I'd prefer to go back to my daydreaming."

The woman sighed. "I . . . I came here wanting to apologize for what I said earlier."

"Which time?"

"The last time. You know, when I said that you *always* arrive a little late."

"So far, I'd have to agree with you."

"I also have to confess that shooting that man has left me somewhat unnerved. That's what I really came to tell you. I've never shot anyone before."

"Comes as no big surprise."

"I thought maybe talking to a man of the gun like yourself would help me sort things out."

"I'm not a 'man of the gun.' I'm a lawman and although I do have to draw my weapon and have killed several outlaws . . . well, more than several, I guess. Anyway, I always try to take my prisoners alive and healthy. It's just that a large percentage of them would rather take their chances shooting it out than going to rot in prison."

"I wouldn't last a month in a prison," she told him. "I'd go crazy if I couldn't be free."

"So would I," Longarm admitted with a passion that surprised even himself. "I might be able to take it for a couple of years, but no more."

"Do you think that we will have any more of the kind of trouble that we've already had in Denver and on this train?"

"Count on it," he told her in a grim voice. "If you and Miss Belcher are determined to travel up to the Comstock Lode and preach for the right of women to vote, even that might not be too bad. But when you add in your condemnation of liquor, well . . . that's like pouring kerosene on a campfire. It's going to explode in our faces."

"The fight to outlaw the devil's drink is something that we believe and *must* do."

"Then it's going to bring us all nothing but grief," Longarm told her without bothering to mince words. "You can't yearn for peace on the one hand and cry out for prohibition on the other. Not in places like Virginia City and Gold Hill where liquor and wild women are a miner's only pleasures."

"Pleasures? What about . . ."

"What?"

"Books!"

"Ha! Most of them can't even read."

"They could learn."

"Lady," he said, "you don't have the faintest notion of what you are talking about. And if you suggest that they could go on hikes or picnics, then I'm just going to laugh my head off and make you even madder."

Katherine blushed with anger or embarrassment. She said nothing for a long time after they had passed the burial hill where Red Killion's bones rested. In fact, they must have traveled another ten or fifteen miles before she managed to say, "The truth of the matter is, if Gertrude would agree to call off touring and lecturing on the Comstock Lode, I really wouldn't be very upset."

He stared at her. "You wouldn't?"

"No."

"Then why don't you—"

"Because other than Constance, I'm the only one who would volunteer to travel West with Gertrude and I just can't abandon her now. If I did, she'd go on alone and probably be shot to death or clubbed or something equally horrendous. If that happened, Marshal, I'd live with guilt the rest of my life."

"Despite what you or I can do, she might be killed anyway," Longarm said. "I'll be very frank with you, Katherine."

"Please do."

"I'm very good at tracking an outlaw down and either finishing him off or bringing him in to justice. I know how to do that real well and it's a straightforward proposition. You know your wanted man and all you have to do is to hunt him down and then either arrest or shoot him. But this is entirely different and fifty times worse."

"I suppose it is."

"No supposin' about it. You see, with this arrangement, I don't have any idea who in a crowd is thinking about murder or mayhem. I can't read minds. If you or Gertrude is standing before a crowd, how am I supposed to know which men among 'em all have killin' in mind?"

"You can't."

"That's right," he said, feeling a little better since she seemed to finally understand his difficult predicament. "If you or Gertrude were the President of these United States, we'd have a whole bunch of people guarding you everywhere you went. But you're *not* that important, and so I have to just do the best that I can."

"You don't inspire my confidence."

"Good!" Longarm exclaimed. "The less confident you are, the more you will watch out for yourselves. Maybe you'll be the first to see a man reach for the gun or knife in his pocket. You protected yourself just the other day on this train, and that gives me hope."

"I think Gertrude is worried."

"She'd better be."

"Marshal, I'll try very hard to talk her out of going up to the Comstock Lode. That's what you want, isn't it?"

"It would be in the best interests of everyone."

"All right," Katherine said, coming to her feet. "I'll start working on that right away. But Gertrude Belcher is incredibly stubborn. If she thinks that I'm out to change her mind, the game is lost. That's why I have to plant little seeds of doubt so she comes to her *own* conclusion that the risks aren't worth the potential rewards."

"Then start planting," Longarm told her, "because there will be no rewards on the Comstock Lode. They'll *never* give up their liquor, their gambling, or their whoring. For most, it's all that they live for from one payday to the next."

"And what about giving women the right to vote?"

"To be truthful, Katherine, there are so few women on the Comstock that I doubt they'd even care. And as a matter of fact, if they thought that giving you a vote would bring more women to Nevada, I expect that they'd be all for the idea."

Katherine Howe almost smiled at that remark, and then she rose and walked away.

Several days later, their train at last reached the outskirts of Reno. The town had originated as an emigrant crossing at the Truckee River called Lake's Crossing. And it might have remained just a small and inconsequential western Nevada settlement had it not been for the Central Pacific Railroad buying up land and then auctioning off lots in the summer of 1868. Charles Crocker, building superintendent of the railroad that had just conquered the Sierra Nevada Mountains, renamed the settlement in honor of General Jesse Reno, a Union officer who had been killed fighting Paiutes six years earlier.

Reno mushroomed thanks to the Central Pacific's great power and popularity. The daily arrival of trains from Sacramento, California, immediately established Reno as the primary distribution center for the fabulously wealthy Comstock Lode as well as western Nevada. While Carson City, Nevada's capital, might be only a day's ride to the south, it was Reno that was well on its way to becoming the state's most important trading and banking center.

Longarm had always enjoyed Reno. Maybe one reason it strongly appealed to him was that, in order to reach it, you had to first cross the miserable Humboldt Sink and the Great Salt Lake Desert. But it was also true that the Truckee, which flowed right through the heart of town, was a fine, good fishing river born of the High Sierras. And finally, the very sight of so much grass, water, and trees was easy on the eye.

"When we were in Salt Lake City," Katherine said, "Gertrude wired ahead to Virginia City that we were coming."

"So she couldn't be talked out of going up on the Comstock," Longarm said with resignation.

"No. I tried and tried, but she wouldn't listen. She believes that wherever the need for reform is greatest, that's where she is supposed to go."

"Like an evangelist, huh?"

"Very much so," Katherine agreed. "Anyway, tonight we are being honored by the Silver State Women's League. It will be inside at the Civic Auditorium, and I don't think that you need to worry about us."

"Why not?"

"Because we will be surrounded by at least a hundred ardent suffragists, and they'd string up any man foolish enough to go inside and even attempt to do us harm."

"What am I supposed to do while you are being feted by all those enlightened women?"

"Take the evening off," Katherine suggested, ignoring his bait.

"You must have friends that you'd like to see."

"As a matter of fact, I do."

"Women friends, I suppose?"

"Yep."

"I thought so." Katherine could not hide her displeasure, and Longarm did not see any point in even discussing the fact that he knew several women of less than sterling reputation who would enjoy his company.

"We'll be staying at the Comstock House on South Virginia Street," she said.

"Nice place," Longarm said. "It's a big two-story brick building just south of the Truckee River. It caters to ladies only. You'll both enjoy your stay."

"We might remain there for several days."

"That would suit me fine."

"Where will you be staying?"

"Close," he promised. "Whenever you and Miss Belcher are out and about, I'll be very near. Sometimes you'll see me, sometimes you won't."

"Will you wear disguises?"

He almost chuckled. "What for?"

"Oh, I don't know. I guess so that if anyone were thinking of doing us harm, they wouldn't realize that you were close by, ready to jump in and offer us protection as well as arrest and throw them in jail."

"Katherine, I *want* anyone of that mind to realize that they're going to have to deal with me before they deal with you. Is that understood?"

"Of course. I was just wondering about your . . . friends."

"I'll be alone when you are out in public, and especially when either of you women are preaching."

"Speaking," she corrected. "We're not preaching."

"I respectfully disagree," Longarm replied. "But we are not going to argue the point."

"Very well. Will you be escorting us to our hotel and to the Civic Auditorium?"

"I will."

"I'm glad."

She started to turn, but he caught her hand, certain that she would jerk it away. He was surprised that she did not. Then, pulling her close, Longarm kissed her gently.

Katherine's eyes widened with shock and surprise. She began to raise her hand, probably to slap his face for such impudence, but then she froze and whispered, "Why did you do that?"

"I just wanted to demonstrate that I'm not all rough bark and rawhide. I can be gentle and kind."

"And so you decided to kiss me?"

"To be honest, I acted entirely on impulse. It wasn't something that I planned. It just happened."

Her head tilted a little. She really did have a pretty face, and if she had used a little color and did something with her hair, Miss Katherine Howe would have been extremely attractive.

"I'm starting to worry myself, Marshal."

"Why?"

"Because I'm beginning to like you."

"And that's so terrible?"

"It is. You see, you *epitomize* the kind of man that I've always abhorred."

"What does that mean?"

"Abhorred means loathed. Intensively disliked."

"Why?"

"Because you are so big and crude and unpolished. You say what you think without much regard for the other person's feelings. You don't want to kill, but you'll do it and not give it much thought afterward."

"I have a conscience," he said, objecting, but not too vigorously. "Don't paint me out to be a dumb, unfeeling brute who acts purely on base instinct."

"I don't think of you that way at all," she whispered, kissing his cheek. "I think you are dangerous, hard, somewhat ruthless, and extremely complex, although you might like to have others suppose you are simple. Marshal, you are also the most exciting and handsomest man I've ever met. You both scare and . . . and thrill me.''

He grinned. "I do?''

"Yes,'' she said, "and that is the scariest part of all.''

Longarm would have liked to explore those feelings in great depth, but he heard the train blast its steam whistle. Then their conductor shouted, "Reno! Reno comin' up in five minutes! Everyone not going on to Sacramento prepare to disembark!''

When Katherine was gone, Longarm gathered up his things and smoothed out his shirt and tie. Katherine didn't wear perfume, but the scent of her was on him anyway. She had a great distrust of men, and Longarm wondered if Katherine was still a virgin.

Longarm found that possibility very . . . arousing.

Chapter 7

Longarm looked in on Gertrude and Katherine, making sure that they were safe at the Comstock House and that local marshals had been assigned for their protection. Satisfied that no harm could come to them, he went looking for fun and diversion. He had not realized it, but the long railroad journey they'd just completed had been something of a strain. A strain because after the shooting incident that had again come so near to claiming Gertrude's life, he had been constantly worried that other maniacs might try to silence the prominent and outspoken suffragist and prohibitionist. He had slept poorly in his railroad sleeping compartment, and even his appetite had suffered.

Now, however, with the two women surrounded by a horde of admirers, and guarded by local marshals who assured him that they would let nothing happen to either woman, Longarm headed for the Pinecone Saloon, which avoided the drunks and the riffraff by charging a bit more for their liquor and by employing a full-time bouncer. The man's only known name was "Buffalo," and he boasted arms the size of most men's legs and the thickest, wildest black beard Longarm had ever seen.

"Marshal Long!" the bouncer exclaimed, extending a hand that could easily crush bones. "Welcome back!"

Buffalo wasn't any taller than Longarm, but he weighed at least three hundred pounds and none of it was fat. The man's strength was legendary, and he was the West's unofficial wrestling and arm-wrestling champion. Buffalo's reputation was so widespread that he could only find opponents by offering lopsided odds, and even then there were few interested in challenging his supremacy. The last man that had tried to whip Buffalo had been a seven-foot-tall Swedish logger from the Pacific Northwest who could bend horseshoes in his bare hands. But after having both of his arms pinned to the table in little more than the blink of an eye, the Swede had challenged Buffalo to a no-holds-barred wrestling match. Buffalo had accepted, but only on the condition that there was no thumbing of eyes or biting off of fingers, ears, noses, or toes.

The contest was still being talked about to this day, and it was said that the pair had wrestled, gouged, kicked, and punched for nearly an hour until Buffalo had dumped the giant in a horse-watering trough and then had jumped on the man's back and held his head underwater until the Swede almost drowned. Yanking the man's head up, Buffalo had slammed and then sawed his neck down against the edge of the trough, breaking his windpipe. They said the Swede had turned purple and that his eyes had bugged almost out of their sockets before he finally managed to suck in an agonizing whiff of breath. It had taken him two months to recover and return to the Pinecone Saloon to pay his debt. After that, he'd slunk back to Washington, but had permanently lost his voice.

"You look mighty fit, Marshal!" Buffalo said, squeezing Custis's hand harder than was necessary. "I'd be willing to give you . . . oh, five-to-one odds that you can't put me down on my back."

Longarm shook his head and grinned, for this was a familiar ritual of words that the man insisted upon. "Hell, Buffalo, you offered me seven-to-one odds the last time I was in town and I was ten pounds heavier then."

"You're probably a lot quicker than me," Buffalo said, licking his porcine lips. "Lean and quick. Why, if you could sort of duck under one of my arms and give me a leg-whip across the back of my knees, I'd *have* to drop and you'd win not only a lot of money, but you'd be famous."

"No, thanks."

"Hell, Marshal, people would stare and whisper your name when you swaggered down the street the same way they do mine."

"The last thing that a good lawman needs is a big reputation to live up to. Buffalo, you're going to have to find yourself another sucker."

"What about fists only? I heard that you pack one hell of a punch. Heard that you broke a man's jaw in a fight with a left uppercut that was too fast for the eye to see.''

''That's just bullshit and beer talk,'' Longarm said. ''Why, I much prefer to pistol-whip some fool than to break my knuckles on his head.''

Buffalo looked discouraged. ''You know, it does get a little boring throwing lesser men out in the street when they get drunk and too rowdy.''

Longarm managed to extract his hand. ''Buffalo, would you listen to a bit of well-meaning advice?''

''I guess.''

Longarm caught the scent of whiskey on Buffalo's breath, and knew that the man was breaking the establishment's rules of not drinking when on duty. ''Go easy on the brag. You know, some day someone *will* whip you. You're not such a young man anymore, and it's gonna happen sooner or later.''

''Be years before I get whipped.''

''I hope so, but when you brag too much, it galls folks. Gall 'em enough and someone might get drunk and crazy enough to put a bullet or a knife in your gizzard.''

''I carry a gun and a knife,'' Buffalo said, pulling back his coat to reveal both weapons. ''But I never have had to use either one of 'em.''

''That's good,'' Longarm said, ''but I'm just trying to tell you not to get too damned cocky, or some little fella might decide that it is worth hanging to have shot and killed the great Reno Buffalo. There are a lot of madmen running loose, and I'd hate to see one of them put you *in* the ground rather than down on it. Savvy?''

''Sure,'' Buffalo said, his face growing serious.

"Why, a little fella that couldn't have weighed more than two hundred pounds tried to knife me a couple weeks back! I broke both of his arms, and then I crushed every damned bone in his knife hand with my boot heel!" Buffalo guffawed lustily. "Why, Marshal, they say he can't even hold his pecker anymore!"

Longarm chose his next words carefully. "You play awfully rough. Maybe too rough."

"And you don't?" the big man challenged. "Why, how many men you killed, Marshal?"

"I dunno. I've been a lawman for a long time."

"Okay, let's make it simple. How many have you killed just in the last year?"

"A couple, I guess, but. . . ."

"Well," Buffalo said, "I never killed *anybody*! Now I come mighty close to killin' that big Swede because he broke the rules we'd agreed to and put a thumb in my right eye. Damn near popped it out like a grape. Yeah, I sorta went crazy. They say the Swede still ain't right in the head on account of not getting any air to his brain for so long. And he can't speak none either. But I never *killed* him. Not like you've killed men."

Longarm nodded in solemn agreement. He knew that Buffalo liked to argue almost as much as he liked to wrestle and brawl. "Say," Longarm said, "is Reba working tonight?"

Buffalo's hands clenched into fists and he had to clear his voice before he growled, "She's working. Came in this morning early and ought to be getting off pretty soon. She'll be tired. You ought to leave her alone."

"Maybe I ought to let her decide how tired she is."

"Marshal, I'm interested in Reba now. Been walking

her home when I can get away from here for a spell. Been walking her down along the river too."

Longarm managed a smile. "That's real nice. You courting Reba?"

"What do you mean?"

"I mean, is it your intention to *marry* her?"

"Hell, no! Just hump her when she's ready. Besides, she wouldn't marry me even if I decided to ask."

"How can you be sure of that?"

"I think Reba is still sweet on *you,* Marshal." Buffalo's eyes squinted, and the first hint of a threat came into his voice. It was surprisingly subtle for such a brutish man, but it was unmistakable, all right. "Marshal, we've always been friends, haven't we?"

"We have," Custis readily agreed.

"Well, then, as one friend to another, I'm askin' you just to stay away from Reba. There's plenty of other wimmen that you could screw when you come to town. But I been walkin' Reba along the river and she's almost my woman now."

"I see."

Longarm *did* see, and the very last thing he wanted to do was to anger Buffalo. Besides, the man was right. There were plenty of women in Reno, and he knew of a couple that might be available on short notice.

"So you stay way away from her," Buffalo ordered, all the friendliness gone from his deep voice. "You hear what I'm tellin' you?"

Longarm might have nodded his head in agreement and done an abrupt about-face if Buffalo hadn't poked him hard in the chest with a forefinger resembling a railroad spike. The poke rocked Longarm back on his heels, and it hurt because it was administered to his breastbone.

Longarm curbed his impulse to draw his gun and use it to part Buffalo's shaggy hair. But they *had* been friends for many years and they'd shared beers, small confidences, and a lot of hearty laughter. That being the case, Longarm allowed the man this indiscretion and said, "If Reba says she's your girl, then that's good enough for me, Buffalo."

Custis began to step around the huge man, but Buffalo grabbed his right bicep with the powerful force of a vise and hissed in his ear, "It don't matter what Reba says, Marshal. It's what *I* say that matters."

Longarm's lips pulled back from his teeth and he snarled, "Let go of my arm."

"You heard me, didn't you?"

"For the last time, let go!"

Buffalo released him and stepped aside. But there was a hardness in his deep-set eyes that Longarm knew spelled big trouble. Ignoring the impulse to set the man straight with his gun barrel, Longarm pushed around him and entered the saloon.

The Pinecone had a small but excellent dining area that served nothing but beefsteak, potatoes, and apple pie. You could order it for breakfast, supper, or dinner, and the smell of the cooking food made him suddenly hungry.

He took a table in the small dining area, and noticed that he was the only one wanting to eat. Checking his Ingersoll pocket watch, Longarm saw that the hour was still early, which explained why the usual crowd was missing.

''Why, Marshal Long!'' Reba exclaimed, hurrying across the room and hugging his neck. ''What a wonderful surprise!''

Longarm couldn't help but grin. Sometimes Reba worked in the saloon, but just as often she cooked in the hot, unventilated kitchen just off the back alley. Now she was cooking, and damp tendrils of blond hair were plastered to her forehead.

Reba was a tall, willowy woman with a stunning smile and magnificent brown eyes. She looked slender and delicate, but Longarm had discovered several years earlier that she was as strong as a puma and more than a little passionate. She had, he remembered, about the most beautiful legs he'd ever seen on a woman, long and tapered and. . . .

''Boy, you look wrung out and worked hard!'' Reba exclaimed, her smile dying as she plopped down in the only other chair at his table. ''You been sick or something?''

''Or something,'' he replied, not really wanting to go into the whole sorry story of how he had been unjustly assigned to guard two women who were rabid prohibitionists and suffragists.

''Well, let's get you a big old steak and some good red California wine to build up your blood! You're almost skinny, Custis! Haven't you been getting enough to eat?''

''I've been traveling a lot and I haven't had any time off for quite a while,'' he told her. ''After this job, I'm going to take a month off and just sip cold beer and swing back and forth all day in a damned hammock slung between a couple of tall pine trees that whisper softly in the wind."

"Why, you always were a poet! I just love the way you describe things so pretty and everything. But a hammock?"

"That's what I said," Longarm replied, feeling a bit foolish. "Anyway, what's wrong with 'em?"

"Nothing! But after I make sure you have the best steak in the house and we stuff you tighter than a tick with potatoes and sourdough bread, I'll take you home to my bed and give you enough lovin' to put you to sleep for two days!"

Ordinarily, Longarm would have laughed. Now, however, the memory and the unmistakable threat of Buffalo was too fresh in his mind, so he said, "Buffalo told me to give you a wide berth. And here we are already talking about going to your bed."

Ordinarily, Reba would have laughed. "Shit! He warned you to stay away from me? He did that?"

"Yep."

Reba spun on her heel and shot out of the dining room. Longarm came out of his chair, but then he eased back down again. He wanted no part of the huge man, but even more relevant was the fact that it was Reba's job—not his—to straighten Buffalo out.

Longarm placed his forearms on the red-and-white checkered tablecloth and let his head droop forward. He *was* tired. Too tired to want any unnecessary trouble. He should have just gone to some other saloon and cafe. He *would* have gone to some other friendly saloon if Buffalo hadn't started to get threatening. But once he'd been threatened, it had become a matter of principle that he enter the Pinecone and enjoy his usual pleasures.

Maybe he dozed for a moment. He must have dozed because the very next thing he knew, Reba came staggering into the dining area with her face smeared with blood. She was dazed, glassy-eyed, and would have collapsed if Longarm hadn't caught her in his arms and eased her down in the chair.

"What happened!" he demanded, already knowing the answer deep inside.

"That big sonofabitch beat hell out of her!" the bartender from the saloon area shouted. "I thought he was gonna kill her before I stuck both barrels in his ugly face!"

Longarm saw that the bartender had a double-barreled shotgun clenched in his fists. And he looked plenty mad enough to use it.

"Marshal!" he shouted. "Buffalo is completely out of control! You got to do something before I kill him!"

"All right," Longarm said, moving past the bartender. "Get Reba some cold compresses and a glass of your best whiskey. I'll take care of Buffalo."

"Here! A single bullet won't stop that monster! You better take my shotgun and you better not hesitate in using it."

For a moment, Longarm actually considered taking the bartender up on his offer. Then, he rejected the idea. A big-gauge shotgun like that, loaded with buckshot and fired at point-blank range, would indeed put a very sudden and definite end to the legend of Buffalo. But the man was drunk and insane with jealousy, and probably deserved to be thrown in a jail rather than a grave.

"Keep the shotgun," Longarm decided, "but if he

puts me down and comes in here after Reba, you blow his belly through his gawdamn backbone, you understand me?''

"You bet I do!'' The bartender looked past Longarm. "Everyone hear that! I got the legal right to kill Buffalo if he comes in here!''

There were a half-dozen patrons that had crowded into the dining area, and they each nodded and then stepped aside as Longarm went stomping through the saloon and out the front door to arrest Buffalo.

Unfortunately, the man was sober enough to anticipate Longarm and act with vicious efficiency. Longarm was just coming through the front door when Buffalo slashed downward with a rough length of two-by-four that struck the barrel of Longarm's pistol and knocked it out of his hands. Then, with a roar, Buffalo swung the two-by-four at Longarm's head with enough force to decapitate him.

Longarm ducked, but not quite enough, as the crown of his hat was leveled and the end of the board splintered against the front of the Pinecone Saloon, shaking the front of the building.

"Drop that board!'' Longarm ordered. "You are under arrest for assault and battery.''

"You better run 'cause in case you haven't noticed, there's no gawdamn gun in your hand!''

Both of them glanced down at Longarm's pistol. Custis wasn't sure, but it appeared that his trusty Colt .44-40 was out of commission.

"I'm lettin' you run for it,'' Buffalo said, the jagged piece of lumber waving back and forth like a finger of death. "You can run with your tail tucked up between your legs . . . or I will skewer you like a pig!"

"Drop the board," Longarm said, ignoring what was probably an excellent suggestion. "You're in enough trouble already, Buffalo. Don't make it worse."

To Longarm's surprise, Buffalo *did* drop the board, but when Longarm started to retrieve his fallen pistol, the bouncer took a menacing step forward saying, "Uh-uh. It's just the two of us with our fists."

"I don't think so," Longarm told him, his hand streaking for a very deadly twin-barreled derringer that was attached to his watch chain instead of the expected fob.

Buffalo stared at the derringer. He looked almost mesmerized, and then he cried, "I told you to just stay away from her! Was that so much to ask of a friend!"

"Yeah," Longarm answered, "because this is a free country. You don't *own* Reba and you don't own me. But worst of all, you knocked the hell out of her and I just hate a gawdamn woman-beater!"

"And I'll whip the shit outta you too!"

Longarm couldn't believe it, but the giant sprang at him with both of those massive hands reaching for the throat. Longarm was up against the door of the saloon, and there was no way that he could duck aside to avoid the charge and almost certainly a broken neck. So he emptied both barrels of the derringer at Buffalo, striking him twice in the chest. Even so, the savageness of Buffalo was so intense that the man kept coming even as the burning hatred in his demented eyes flickered like the flame of a miner's candle.

Longarm tried to bring the derringer up and slam it into the mass of beard that covered the lower half of

Buffalo's face. He braced himself for impact, and the huge man nearly crushed his chest as they crashed through the door and went spilling back into the saloon.

Buffalo was dying, but it was a titanic death driven by primordial mania. Thick fingers clawed like tentacles reaching for Longarm's windpipe. And they would have squashed it had Longarm not managed to stab the smoking barrel of his empty derringer into Buffalo's right eye and twist the hard steel into the pulpy flesh of the orbit until Buffalo expended the last shred of his inhuman strength screaming curses.

The stunned patrons had to pull Buffalo's body off Longarm, for he had not the strength to do so himself. They had to pick Longarm up and practically carry him to a chair and then pour whiskey down his gullet until the liquor burned away an oppressive fog that seemed unwilling to clear from behind his eyes.

"Jaysus Kee-rist!" someone cried in a tone that bordered on hysteria. "Marshal, even with two .44-caliber slugs in his chest, he almost kilt ya!"

"Yeah," Longarm wheezed. "How is Reba?"

"She's gettin' drunk. Keeps trying to come out here and fight, though."

"The fighting is over for tonight," he said, pushing himself up and hanging onto the table with one hand and his whiskey bottle with the other. "Help me back to the dining room. I got a steak on the stove."

They escorted Longarm through the saloon and eased him down at the same table beside Reba. They stared at each other. Then Longarm finally broke the silence by saying, "Dear Reba, do I look as bad as you?"

"I don't think so," she replied between puffy lips and

with her eyes nearly swollen shut. "Why don't we go to my place, get in bed and get drunk, then just sleep."

"Sounds good to me," he said, knowing that making love tonight was the very last thing that he or Reba wanted . . . or needed.

"You got any more boyfriends that possess the strength of a grizzly bear?" Longarm asked when they reached her room and staggered inside.

"No. You're the next-biggest one I got."

Longarm unbuckled his gun and flopped on her bed. "I ain't even gonna undress."

"No need to. Nothin' is gonna happen but us sleepin'."

He nodded. Tomorrow, he'd have to go to local authorities and fill out a ream of paperwork explaining why a federal officer had killed a local citizen. It was a bother, and it had been a clear-cut matter of self defense. Buffalo would have broken him in half. It was too bad the man had to die, Longarm thought, but far better him than Reba or me.

Chapter 8

Longarm woke up in an angry mood, and the pounding at his door shortly after daybreak did nothing to improve his mood.

"Who is it?"

"Marshal Ben Horton! Open up, Marshal Long. We've got some business to attend to about last night's fatal shooting!"

"Can't it wait? Gawdamn it, there were dozens of witnesses that can give you the same story."

"Rise and shine, Marshal. You too, Reba."

Longarm rolled out of bed. He grabbed his pants and had a hell of a time pulling them on as he hopped to the door. Opening it, he peered out to see Horton standing at attention with a grim expression on his round face. "Marshal Horton, we're gonna have some breakfast and coffee before we come over and make a report on that shooting."

"I'm sorry, but I've got appointments all morning and we need to get this business finished before my day gets too hectic. How is Reba?"

"She's pretty well beat up," Longarm replied.

"Yeah," Horton said, "that's what I'd heard. Sorry to have to roust you both out of bed so early, but a man has been killed and the fact that he deserved it doesn't change the paperwork."

"I know," Longarm said. "Why don't we meet in about a half hour over at Barney's Cafe?"

"That would be fine. I haven't eaten yet."

"Okay, then order us both a big breakfast and have your paperwork ready."

"Sounds good to me," Horton said. "But don't keep me waiting too long."

"I won't," Custis promised, closing the door.

He hated to drag Reba out of her bed so early, but there was no help for it. Her pretty face was mottled with purple, and her lips were caked with blood and badly swollen. Like Longarm, the woman was not in a good mood.

"Couldn't the sonofabitch have waited just a few more hours before we have to give him the details that he's probably already heard from twenty or thirty people!" Reba wailed.

"No," Longarm replied, "and the very fact that everyone in town will be giving him a different version of the shooting makes it all the more important that we set the record straight."

Reba tottered over to the vanity and stared at herself

in the mirror. "Oh, my God! I'm not setting foot out of this room until I look human again!"

In truth, Longarm couldn't blame her. Normally, she was a damned attractive woman, but she wouldn't be again for at least another week. Still, Longarm knew Marshal Horton would insist on seeing her this morning and getting his reports taken care of without delay.

"Do you have a veil or anything?"

"Of course not!"

"Reba, you *have* to come out this morning."

"No, I don't," she said, clenching her fists at her sides. "You may not live in this town, but *I do*. And I'm not going to have everyone seeing me look like this."

"All right," Longarm said. "I'll explain things to Marshal Horton and ask him to put it off for a day or two. After all, I'm the one that killed Buffalo."

"Thanks," she said. "If he insists on talking to me today, he'll have to break down my door, and you can tell him that I'll shoot him and claim he was a rapist."

It was a joke, and Reba tried to laugh, but it hurt too much.

His session with Marshal Horton went smoothly. Horton was an experienced lawman who didn't waste either his own time or anyone else's with silly questions. The reports were pretty straightforward, and they took less than fifteen minutes to complete. After several cups of coffee and a stack of flapjacks drenched in maple syrup, Longarm was feeling half human again.

"I'm sorry that you had to be the one to kill Buffalo," Horton said. "He was getting worse lately and getting pretty vicious. After what he did to that big Swede a while back, I knew the time would come when I'd have to deal with the man."

"Well," Longarm said, "you can't do much until a crime has been committed."

Horton seemed lost in his own thoughts. "Frankly, the man scared me and my deputies. I mean, we *knew* that the day would come when we'd have to arrest Buffalo, and we figured that would be the day when some of us would get hurt . . . or worse. I owe you a favor, Marshal Long. He was on his way to killing someone, and it could have been Reba."

"He was real jealous."

"Oh, you bet he was! And everyone in this town knew that they had better not get close to Reba or they were just asking for trouble."

"She asked if you could wait a day or two to interview her," Longarm told the man. "She looks pretty bad with her face all discolored and swollen."

"Ah," Horton grunted with a wave of his hand, "I've got all the information that I need. I doubt that she'll be attending Buffalo's funeral."

"Will anyone?"

"Yet bet! He was a legend. A legend going sour, maybe, but a legend all the same. Why, he had the strength of ten men! I've seen him do things that I would have never believed any human could do."

"He always wanted to beat me at something," Longarm said. "Maybe if I had arm-wrestled and lost to him, he wouldn't have gone so crazy last night."

"I doubt it," Horton countered. "The man was like a volcano waiting to erupt. Sooner or later, some poor ignorant bastard would have gotten too close to Reba and Buffalo would have finished him off.''

''I suppose.''

''What about them women suffragists?''

''What about them?''

''Well,'' Horton said, ''I've had two deputies assigned to them and they seem as peaceable as lambs. Both gave speeches last night to a roomful of ladies, and are attending a luncheon at the Mapes Hotel today at noon. Do you really think that they need full-time protection?''

''Yes, they do,'' Longarm answered, telling the man about what had happened on the steps of the Denver Mint as well as on the train coming west. He ended up by saying, ''They sure don't want trouble, but when you start telling people to ban liquor, you are talking about something very near and dear to the Western man regardless of whether he works in a mine or on a horse.''

''Okay,'' Horton said, ''I'll keep them under our protection. But I can't really spare the men. How long are they planning to be in Reno?''

''I expect them to leave tomorrow,'' Longarm said.

''Good!'' Horton stood up and gathered his paperwork. ''Well, Marshal, I wish you all the best on the Comstock Lode. You know that the message of prohibition and women voting isn't going to be popular.''

''I know. But our Constitution guarantees them the right to freedom of speech, and they're not going to be silenced given how strongly they believe in their message.''

''I'm glad that I'm just a lowly town marshal,'' Horton said with a wink. "This way, I get to avoid these kinds of assignments."

"You sure do. Don't suppose that you could offer me a job, could you?"

Horton chuckled. "I know you well enough to figure you'd be bored and restless always confined to the Reno city limits. Nope, you're perfectly well suited to doing your job and I'm not half bad at mine. If possible, stop by for a minute to let me know when you are leaving."

"So long, Marshal," Longarm said, motioning for a final cup of coffee as Horton left.

He was halfway through it when he realized someone was standing behind him. Longarm twisted around to see Katherine Howe, and managed to form a smile and say, "Good morning. Care to join me for breakfast?"

She sat down without a smile and said, "I heard that you shot a man to death last night in a saloon."

"I had to do it in order to save my own neck. What is it to you anyway?"

"Gertrude was very upset to hear the news."

"Sorry to hear that," Longarm replied. "But again, what business is it of hers . . . or yours?"

"You were assigned to protect *us*."

"I know. And as soon as I finish this cup of coffee, I was about to go over and look in on you."

"How thoughtful."

Longarm took a deep breath and tried not to lose his temper. In his nicest possible manner, he asked, "Have we got a problem?"

"I think that we do."

"Spell it out plain for me."

"You were involved in a *saloon* shooting last night in which a very famous man was killed."

"Oh, he wasn't *that* famous."

"There could be publicity! And how would that look, you drinking and involved in a killing while you're supposed to protect us!"

"If I had shot Buffalo in the street instead of a saloon, would that have looked better for you and Gertrude?"

"Yes!" She colored with anger. "I mean . . . well, perhaps! But we don't need this kind of publicity."

"I'll try not to kill anyone else in a saloon while I'm on the assignment," he said, not bothering to hide his sarcasm. "Is that good enough?"

She turned to leave, but not before saying, "We would like to go up to the Comstock Lode and stay tonight in Virginia City."

"Tonight!"

"Yes. Gertrude feels very badly about the fact that you were a party to a saloon killing. She intends to get Marshal Horton's deputies to continue to guard us up on the Comstock Lode."

"And what am I supposed to do?"

"Why don't you just go get drunk again with that saloon slut that you were with all last night and over whose attentions a man died?"

"Oh," Longarm said, jumping up from his table and spilling his coffee. "So *that* is what is *really* bothering you, isn't it! You're not so upset about the shootout or about me killing Buffalo. You're furious because it was over a woman that I happen to like and spent the night with!"

"You go to Hell!" Katherine shouted as she hurried out the front door.

Longarm returned to his table and angrily motioned for another cup of coffee and some towels to soak up the spilled mess. Women! They were impossible.

"Couldn't help but overhear that," the middle-aged waitress said. "If I were you, I'd tell that witch to jump on her broom and try to ride it off a mountaintop."

The remark tickled Longarm's fancy, and he actually laughed out loud. "I'll tell her that someday," he answered.

Fifteen minutes later, however, he was on his way to the Comstock House to have a showdown with the suffragists. First and foremost, they had no authority to replace him with local lawmen. And secondly, he was irreplaceable. Admittedly, he had not been that effective in fending off their attackers and detractors. But the real work was yet to begin up on the Comstock Lode and, if they were to survive, they would need the very best protection and that meant Marshal Custis Long.

"Morning, Marshal Long," a kid selling papers on the street corner called, rushing over. "Can I have your autograph!"

"What for?"

"You're *famous*! You're the man that kilt Buffalo!"

"I want no fame, especially for causing the death of another man."

"But it was you that shot him dead! Please, Marshal Long! Before everyone else comes running and I got no chance to ask you for your autograph."

Longarm felt foolish, but he signed the scrap of paper that the kid held out. Then he hurried on. He had not reached the Truckee Bridge Crossing before he was surrounded by others also wanting to shake his hand and get his autograph.

It was enough to make a grown lawman weep.

Chapter 9

When Longarm arrived at the Comstock House, he was met by a pair of local marshals, one of whom was Ben Horton, who held up his hand and said, "Now hold up a minute, Marshal. You can't just go barging inside."

"Oh, yes, I can," Longarm said, coming to a halt. "I am responsible for guarding Miss Belcher and Miss Howe, and that's exactly what I'm going to do until I hear from my superiors in Denver that I should do otherwise."

"I don't give a damn about your 'superiors,' " Horton said, an edge creeping into his voice. "All I know is that I just received a telegram from Governor Thompson, and he requested that me and my deputies take over *your* job until both those ladies have left Nevada. I guess he figures that we don't need the kind of bad publicity that them getting killed or attacked would give our state.''

Longarm raised his eyebrows in question. ''That's odd because just this morning over breakfast I seem to remember that you told me—''

''Yeah, I know what I told you,'' Horton snapped. ''But that was before I got a telegram from the very same governor who got me my job in the first place.''

''Now I see what's going on,'' Longarm grated out. ''You're just being used by some tinhorn politician.''

Horton flushed. ''Seems to me that the pot is callin' the kettle black.''

Longarm took a deep breath. There was no denying that Marshal Horton was right. Longarm was being used by Colorado politicians.

''You know what I think I'm going to do?'' Longarm said, quickly reaching a decision.

''Nope.''

''I'm going to go up to the Comstock Lode and keep an eye on those ladies.''

''That won't be necessary. I'm taking this on personally, and I'm bringing up two of my best deputies to help. The thing of it is, Marshal, thosc two women will have far better protection than you gave 'em.''

''That's your opinion,'' Longarm said. ''And I'm doing what I was asked to do by my Denver office and that's to stay with them. Now, you wouldn't have any foolish notions about trying to order me to stay away from our Eastern lady friends, would you, Marshal?''

Horton chuckled. ''Hell, no, I wouldn't do that! After all, it's a free country and . . . oh, excuse me. I've got some newspaper people from Sacramento and Carson City that are begging me for an exclusive interview. Something about how I feel concerning woman's suffrage and prohibition.''

''How *do* you feel?''

''Just between me and you, I think women ought to stay home and tend the fire,'' Horton said under his breath and with a big smile. ''And I think they ought to allow a man to enjoy the *second* greatest pleasure in his life, and maybe they should even drink to his health.''

Horton laughed out loud a moment before he began to smooth his hair and then straighten his tie. It was clear to see that the Reno lawman was not only influenced by the governor, but also by his own vanity.

Marshal Horton began shaking hands and then posing for pictures. It was all too much for Longarm, so he headed for the telegraph office. He needed to update Billy Vail and request his authority to continue this assignment despite the fact that the suffragists had unceremoniously dumped him. There was little doubt that Billy would be incensed and order Longarm up to Virginia City. Any way he looked at this situation, it had become a high-stakes chess game between politicians, meaning that he and Ben Horton were simply a couple of expendable pawns.

A short time later, Longarm sent one of the longest telegrams of his professional career. He outlined everything that had happened on his watch since leaving Denver with the two women, and ended by asking what was now expected.

Billy's answer came back within an hour and read:

YOU ARE IN CHARGE OF THEIR SAFETY **STOP** STAY WITH THEM UNTIL THEY LEAVE THE WEST **STOP** DON'T EVER RETURN HERE IF THEY ARE KILLED BY ASSASSINS **STOP** INFORM ME WHEN YOU GET TO VIRGINIA CITY AND STAY IN TOUCH EVERY DAY **STOP** DON'T MESS THIS UP OR WE WILL BOTH GET THE AX **STOP**

Longarm laughed out loud when he read that telegram. It confirmed what he had expected, and although only yesterday he would have jumped at the chance to quit this assignment and return to Denver, today he was of an entirely different mind. His pride was stung, and he didn't like the way that any of this was unfolding, especially the way that Marshal Horton was gobbling up the publicity like a hog at the trough.

Longarm sent a short telegram back to Billy informing him that he was on his way to the Comstock Lode, but that he would need and expected some additional travel funds to be ready and waiting when he arrived, because the Comstock was expensive and he had no intention of living in some canvas tent with a bunch of drunken and injured miners.

He stopped off to explain things and say good-bye to Reba, who had gone straight back to bed. "I'm sorry the way this all worked out," Longarm told the battered woman. "I wish that . . ."

Reba put a finger up to press his lips into silence. "Shhh . . . you may be sorry, but I'm not. Oh, sure, I look like hell right now, but I'll be much better tomorrow, and in a week or two I'll be as good as ever."

"Of course you will. You're a beautiful woman."

"And you are a handsome man," she said. "When I get pretty again, I'm going to come up to Virginia City and—"

"I'll probably be gone by then," Longarm interrupted. "My guess is that the miners up there will be so rowdy that the suffragists won't even have a chance to be heard. I expect them to be chased off in a day or two."

"Then come back down here and we'll take care of some long-overdue business," Reba said. "You may feel bad about what Buffalo did to my face, but I say it was well worth a couple of shiners and smashed lips to have you gun the bastard down. I think I got off real lucky."

"I'm glad that you feel that way."

"You want some right now?"

Longarm was shocked. "I couldn't do that! Not with you all banged up."

"Sure you could," Reba said, boldly rubbing the crotch of his pants.

"I'd hurt you."

Reba shook her head. "Take your pants off and come into me from behind."

He couldn't help grinning. "You mean it?"

"Sure!"

Longarm felt his throat go a little dry. He watched as Reba climbed out of bed and then removed her nightgown to reveal that beautiful body. A moment later, she bent over at the waist and spread her lovely legs far apart.

"Come on, Custis, you know you want it bad."

He *did* want it, and Reba was right. Longarm could

see no reason why he couldn't have her this way and avoid any touching of her injured face.

"You got me pegged," Longarm said as he unbuckled his gunbelt and slung it over the bedpost.

"No," she said, "you're about to get *me* pegged."

Longarm tore off his boots and then his pants. He was already stiff and aroused. When Reba wiggled her bottom, he stepped in close behind, and then bent a little at the knees and discovered that she was aroused too.

'You're already wet, Reba!"

"I've been thinking about this since last night," she answered, moaning softly as his manhood entered her from behind. "Haven't done it this way for a long time. Can't imagine why not, though. It feels *ever* so fine!"

Longarm thought so too. He and Reba were both tall and they fit together perfectly. He placed his hands on her shapely hips and began to row them back and forth to his own driving rhythm, until they were banging together like a couple of runaway boxcars racing down a mountainside.

"Oh," Reba cried, her legs starting to shake as Longarm pounded up into her harder and harder. "Oh, honey!"

Longarm's lips pulled back from his teeth and he could feel the fire building hotter and hotter, until it erupted like a volcano and he pumped his seed way up into Reba. At the same instant, he felt her own bottom begin to twitch as she also lost control, grabbing her breasts and crying out in ecstacy and then sagging as he held her impaled on his massive rod and finished his pleasuring.

Longarm had to carry Reba back to the bed, and for

just a moment, he felt guilty for allowing himself to be talked into screwing.

"That was *so* good, Custis," she breathed.

"You can say that again."

"When you come back down from the Comstock, even if it's as early as tomorrow, you come see me and we'll do it again a time or two. Okay?"

"You bet," he answered, crawling back into his pants.

"And please be careful up there. I don't have to tell you that the Comstock Lode is the home of a lot of crazy, desperate men."

"Marshal Horton and two of his deputies will be helping me protect Gertrude and Katherine," Longarm said. "There's nothing for me to worry about."

"Of course there is," Reba argued. "If there wasn't, then you wouldn't be leaving my bedside for at least a few more days."

"That's true enough," Longarm agreed. "Especially after finding out how much pleasure we can still give each other."

Longarm left Reba and headed for the Truckee Stagecoach Company yard, where he knew that several coaches a day were shuttling between Reno and Virginia City. He bought himself a ticket, and damned if he didn't have to sign a bunch of autographs for the company's employees as well as five other passengers also waiting to go up to the Comstock Lode.

"I don't much enjoy this," he confided to the stage company owner, a man name Pete Owens. "I work best when no one knows me or the nature of my business."

"I can understand that," Owens said. "But like it or

not, you are the man that shot and killed Buffalo. I expect that once they find out in Virginia City that it was you that gunned him down, they'll hound you for autographs up there too.''

''Be obliged if no one tells them of the fact.''

''Sorry,'' Owens answered, ''but like it or not, you *are* famous. Funny thing is, I've just rented a special coach to Marshal Horton and a couple of his deputies who are going to take that other famous person. Her name is . . . oh, dammit, I can't remember.''

''It's Gertrude Belcher and—''

''That's right! Hatchet Belcher! There's another woman going along. Haven't met her, though. She's probably just as old and ugly as Hatchet.''

''Not exactly,'' Longarm said. ''When is that 'special coach' leaving?''

''Marshal told me to have it ready to go by five o'clock this afternoon.''

Longarm was relieved because his stagecoach was leaving two hours earlier. That way, he could call on the telegraph office to collect his additional travel funds and have time to find a good hotel and have a meal before the suffragists arrived.

Would they see him watching over them? Of course. Would they feel any safer or be glad that he had refused to give up his Denver assignment? No.

None of that mattered. The important thing to Longarm was that he had given his word to Billy Vail that he would see this job out to the bitter end so they both could keep their jobs. That mattered a lot. Especially to Billy, who had a wife and children to feed.

''Marshal Long?''

He turned around to see a freckled kid with bare feet standing in front of a horde of dusty little heathens. They were all grinning with unconcealed excitement.

"Yes?"

"Would you tell us *exactly* how you gunned down Buffalo last night?"

"No," Longarm replied. "I didn't want to kill Buffalo. I wanted to arrest him."

"Why?"

"Because that is what a good lawman does," Longarm explained, suspecting that his message was not getting across. "Anyone can draw a gun and shoot another man down. It's a lot harder and more difficult to arrest him and avoid bloodshed."

"You must have been scared shitless," the freckled kid said, eyes round with wonder. "Why, everyone in town figured it'd take a cannon ball to stop Buffalo."

"They were wrong," Longarm said. "No matter how big and strong a man is, he can't stand up to a couple of .44-caliber slugs. It was a sad thing that I had to do. Buffalo just went crazy and he gave me no choice."

"They say them two slugs from your derringer didn't stop him and that he kept coming and almost broke your neck!" another of the kids exclaimed. "Is that really true, Marshal Long?"

Custis gave up and said, "Yeah, that is true. He was the most powerful man I ever faced. It's a shame that all that strength was wasted."

"We saw him wrestle the Swede!" a small boy with buck teeth cried. "Saw him almost drown that big sonofabitch and then saw his damned neck plumb off!"

"You're too young to cuss," Longarm said with a

frown. ''And why aren't you boys in school learning something that will help you make your way in life?''

''Hell,'' the big one said, ''there's no school today 'cause it's Saturday!''

''Oh, yeah.''

''Can we each have your autograph? Please!''

Longarm wasn't pleased. He looked over the heads of these ragamuffins and saw Owens grinning at him with his own fresh autograph. ''I guess.''

After that, more and more kids kept coming. It was like some kind of invisible wire was running from this bunch to every other bunch of Reno boys. And that was the way Longarm had to spend his time until his stage was ready to roll for Virginia City.

''If you want my advice,'' Owens said a moment before Longarm climbed aboard the stage, ''you'll forget about trying to be anonymous and enjoy your celebrity!''

Longarm wasn't buying that. You only had to think of how other famous lawmen had gotten killed for their celebrity. Men like Wild Bill Hickock, who had been assassinated by a coward while playing poker in a Dakota boomtown called Deadwood.

No, sir! Fame and notoriety for a lawman was a ready invitation for some lowly bastard to become famous himself, even if it meant a trip to the gallows.

Chapter 10

Because Longarm had often visited Virginia City, the "Queen of the Comstock Lode," he knew that the mining town had gotten its name when a drunken prospector named James Finney had stumbled and smashed his whiskey bottle on a rock. Looking up and attempting to salvage some semblance of dignity, Finney had proclaimed to his hooting friends, "By gawd, I christen this place Old Virginny!"

No one knew exactly what had happened to James Finney. Certainly the man had never suspected that the site he had christened would one day become a world-famous boomtown. The town had begun as an ordinary tent city clinging to the harsh wind-whipped slopes of Sun Mountain. With precious little water to spare, the earliest prospectors had panned a curious "blue muck," which was finally recognized to be high-grade silver.

Soon after that, the excited miners had learned that an immense vein of pure silver plunged downward following the general directions of Gold Hill and Six-Mile Canyons.

This was to be a hardrock mining town in the truest sense. Tunneling began in earnest as investors and miners alike flocked to the Comstock Lode. Longarm knew that many of the earliest, luckiest, and wisest like George Hearst, Adolph Sutro, Henry Comstock, and Sandy Bowers had become fabulously rich. From its humble beginnings, Virginia City, as well as its envious neighbors Gold Hill and Silver City, had flourished and become world famous as a mecca for hardrock miners as well as entrepreneurs, con artists, prostitutes, and card sharks.

The Comstock Lode was now an immense mining sector where dozens of mine shafts powered by gigantic steam engines lowered men and equipment in steel cages almost two thousand feet into the hot depths of Sun Mountain in order to extract fortunes. Longarm had been down in those hellish depths, but never for long. In the deepest caverns where miners swarmed like ants, the temperatures were well over one hundred and twenty degrees and disastrous cave-ins were commonplace. The Comstock Lode was less than a quarter century old, but its cemeteries were large and growing.

"What brings you up here, Marshal Long?" a plump and sweating whiskey salesman named Givens cheerfully asked. "Say, Marshal, are you after someone else to shoot up in Virginia City? If you are, I'd like to watch."

When Longarm said nothing, Givens added with a

snorting laugh, "I sure wouldn't want to get too close, though!"

The coach was crowded, and the climb up to Virginia City was steep and precarious, with many hairpin turns and plunging drop-offs into waterless canyons far below. Longarm was in no mood for pleasantries, and replied curtly, "A lawman's business is his *own* business, and I intend to keep it that way."

"Well, gosh almighty!" Givens blustered, looking shocked and insulted. "You don't have to be snippy about it just because you got famous by killing Buffalo!"

"Why don't you just enjoy the view and leave me in peace?" Longarm suggested.

"I just thought—"

"Why don't you be quiet," a reed-thin passenger of indeterminate age and profession suggested in a whispery voice, "Marshal Long isn't interested in conversation, and your question was both rude and insulting."

"Who asked you!" Givens demanded, blustering at someone even less physically imposing than himself. "Why, you look like a tubercular!"

In response, the thin man coughed in Givens's face without even bothering to cover his mouth. The whiskey peddler recoiled against his seat and covered his mouth with a dirty silk handkerchief. "Dammit! You had no right to do that! Marshal, he could be a lunger and we might all catch tuberculosis and die!"

"Cover your mouth," Longarm ordered the thin man. "And please keep it shut, especially if you are tubercular."

"I'm not," the man said with great dignity. "I'm an

undertaker and I am answering a newspaper ad for employment. I hear that the funeral business is brisk on the Comstock Lode.''

''That it is,'' Longarm said, secretly relieved that this man was not carrying that fatal and widespread affliction. ''And I would guess that there are already at least four undertakers at work in Virginia City alone.''

''The ad was for Silver City. I was informed by the driver that it is only a few miles beyond Virginia City and over a ridge called The Divide.''

''That's right,'' Longarm said. ''You can walk out of Virginia City, then over The Divide, and on down to Silver City. It can't be more than a mile or two.''

''I don't like to walk,'' the undertaker informed him. ''How many cemeteries are there on the entire Comstock Lode?''

''At least four big ones that I know about.''

''I hope that they are segregated.''

The remark irritated Longarm, who knew that many cemeteries across America were segregated according to race. There were almost always separate cemeteries for Indians, Mexicans, Chinese, and Negroes. Protestants, Jews, and Catholics were usually buried in gated and exclusive sections as if their occupants' bones could discern the ancestry of those rotting nearby. The whole concept of segregated burials was ridiculous as far as he was concerned.

''There are four cemeteries in Virginia City and one more each in Gold Hill and Silver City,'' a well-dressed and prosperous-looking businessman informed everyone. ''But you may be shocked and annoyed to learn that many miners are simply thrown down abandoned mine shafts.''

''My Gawd!'' the undertaker exclaimed. ''How crude and inhuman! Why—''

''The miners come from all over the country as well as the world,'' the businessman explained. ''Many of them have lost contact with their families and die penniless. Their friends are always broke as well, and would much rather spend their money on a drunken wake than hand it over to an undertaker who will charge dearly for his services and a decent coffin.''

''Absolutely barbaric!''

''Maybe so,'' the man answered, ''but no one up here worries much about manners or appearances. Tossing a body down a mine shaft and then getting drunk and pitching in stones and gravel to cover a friend up is very common, not to mention expedient.''

The undertaker shook his head. ''The ad that ran in the Sacramento paper said nothing about this barbaric practice. It's really outrageous and unheard of!''

''There are a lot of things that are unheard of up here, mister.'' The businessman wagged his finger at the undertaker. ''I suggest you get used to them in a hurry.''

''I don't think I'm going to like this Comstock Lode,'' the undertaker said, peering out the stagecoach window. ''It is barren and ugly! No pines, no grass, no *greenery* like we have in California.''

''If I were you,'' Givens said, ''I'd go right back to California. You don't sound like the kind of man that will stick it out more than a few weeks up here. I expect this climate is too harsh for you.''

The two began to quarrel until Longarm shouted,

"Would you both shut up! We'll be in Virginia City in just a couple of hours and I'll be damned if I am going to listen to you people bickering all the way!"

Givens and the unhappy undertaker fell silent, and Longarm's mind drifted. He had many friends in Virginia City. One of his best friends was the tall and sardonic William Wright, who had become prominent writing under the pen name of Dan De Quille. De Quille had once been good friends with a fellow reporter named Samuel Clemens, who had adopted the now-famous alias Mark Twain as his pen name. It was while working together for the *Territorial Enterprise* that the two men had earned their reputations as being astute reporters as well as great humorists.

"There it is," the businessman said, sticking his arm out of the window and pointing to the world-famous boomtown just up ahead.

The first sight of Virginia City was always impressive. Maybe it was because the surrounding landscape was so harsh and forbidding that you found it nearly impossible to believe that anyone would come up there to live and to build. Yet buildings numbered in the thousands. Most impressive were the immense mining operations, which were easily identifiable by their smokestacks and great tin-covered buildings protecting the powerful hoisting works that were the very heart of every mining operation. These mammoth tin buildings were almost always built on a hillside, and were accompanied by immense mounds of crushed rock called "tailings" that were the debris brought out of the earth and then dumped down the hillsides after being rendered worthless. It was the opinion of most mining experts that these discards or tailings were so latently rich in cast-off gold dust and flakes of silver that, someday, advances in extraction technology would make them extremely valuable.

"I had no idea it would be so big," a man who had been silent the entire journey whispered. "What is the population?"

"It varies depending on how the stock market and the mines are doing," the businessman said. "When things are going well and the mines are operating at full employment, meaning they are running three shifts and never close, then the population is around forty thousand, though it's impossible to get a really accurate count since so many are foreigners and refuse to be included in a census. But I'd say that the Comstock Lode is at least forty thousand and maybe nearer to fifty."

"That's amazing!"

The whiskey peddler said, "People come up here for only one reason—money. Money and what it will buy in the saloons and whorehouses. They usually come penniless and leave the same way, but often only after their dreams are shattered and their health is broken."

"Ah!" the businessman scoffed. "You sound like *you* ought to be the undertaker. People come up here for more reasons than women and money. They come up for adventure and excitement! They come up to see famous actors and actresses at our Piper's Opera House. They come up to breathe the sage and build our new Virginia and Truckee Railroad. They come up to be a part of the greatest boomtown in America!"

"You must be a patron of the Chamber of Commerce," Givens said.

"As a matter of fact, I'm a city councilman and former mayor! Now I promote Virginia City and work for the new Virginia and Truckee Railroad. The V&T, gentlemen! It runs from Carson City right up to Virginia City, and turned a profit in its very first year. It carries hopes and it carries precious ore, mining machinery, and the lifeblood of the Comstock, which is its courageous citizens.''

The undertaker rolled his eyes, and the whiskey peddler looked bored. Longarm curbed an urge to inform the businessman that all mining towns eventually died. Sooner or later, every one of them ran out of ore to mine, and then they went bust in a big hurry. He'd seen the pattern a hundred times in a hundred places and in his opinion, the bigger and richer the ore strike, the greater the fall when the mines inevitably ran out of precious ore.

They rolled up C Street past the infamous Bucket of Blood Saloon on the left and the Silver Dollar Saloon on the right. There were dozens of other saloons, but those were a couple of the best. Looking eastward out through the big windows of the Bucket of Blood, Longarm and his friends had spent many a happy hour studying hundreds of miles of empty brown mountains and valleys. And Longarm was quite sure that every one of them was being prospected in the hope that they would become the next Big Bonanza.

''Virginia City!'' the driver shouted as their stage made a sharp right and pulled up the steep grade to the next highest thoroughfare, which was B Street. ''Everybody prepare to unload and hang onto your wallets!''

It was meant as a joke, but every newcomer with any sense at all took it as a warning. Thieves, pickpockets, and armed thugs were in abundance, and they could have your money and your life in a moment and then easily disappear into the crowded city to find another unwary victim. Furthermore, two of the favorite places for these predators to hang out and choose easy marks were at the V&T Railroad or this stage station. Longarm knew for a fact that he and all his fellow passengers would be carefully scrutinized as they disembarked. Anyone looking like he had a few dollars would be considered good pickings.

"You watch yourself," Longarm warned the undertaker. "Stay with the crowds and don't go walking about alone until you get the feel of this town."

"Why?"

"Because you'll get robbed," Longarm said bluntly.

The undertaker looked around, and now he saw a few men watching him with unconcealed interest. "Marshal, my name is Steven Fishburn. Do you mind if I walk with you a ways?"

"Of course not."

Longarm gave the thieves that were studying Fishburn a hard look. He even pointed a warning finger to one of them who he knew to be especially bold. His warning seemed to have a positive effect because the thugs drifted away.

"I really appreciate you doing this," Fishburn said, looking extremely relieved.

"No problem."

"I don't suppose I could prevail upon your good nature to walk me down to Silver City."

"Nope."

"What if I paid you . . . two dollars?"

"I'm sorry," Longarm told the man as they both gathered their bags. "I'm not here to have a nice vacation. I've a job to do."

Fishburn gulped. "But wouldn't that include protecting an honest citizen?"

"Look. If you're that worried, why don't I walk you over to the marshal's office, where you can try and talk someone into escorting you to Silver City. I'm sure that they'd do it for a dollar or two."

"I . . . I suppose that would work."

"Sure! Or else, why don't you just go into the stage line office and wait until the next coach heads back to Reno? No offense, Mr. Fishburn, but I really don't think you belong on the Comstock Lode."

"I quite agree." Fishburn cleared his throat. "Unfortunately, I . . . I don't have quite enough money for the necessary coach fare to get me back to Reno."

"You're almost broke?"

"Actually," Fishburn said, "I was held up last night in Reno after having my dinner and then going for a walk to ease my indigestion."

"So," Longarm said, "are you down to your last couple of dollars?"

"Nearly," Fishburn admitted, looking completely downcast. "I don't like it up here, but I do need that job. I already looked in Reno and there is nothing available. People don't die in Reno or Sacramento with the high frequency that they seem to die up here on the Comstock Lode."

"That's not too surprising."

"It's why I am determined to go to the Silver City. I have few alternatives. I thought about trying my hand at mining, but I doubt that I could stand up to the physical punishment.''

''You're right.''

''So what can I do!'' Fishburn cried with panic rising in his voice. ''Standing here, I feel like a fish among sharks. I believe I appear vulnerable and will get assaulted.''

''Are you unarmed?''

''Of course! I've never owned a gun, much less fired one.''

''Too bad. Sometimes, they come in real handy.''

''Yes, I'm sure that they do, especially among this riffraff. My fear is that when a ruffian discovers that I only have two dollars and some change, he might get very angry and shoot me dead.''

Fishburn's eyes misted. ''Being a stranger and without any money even for my own poor burial, they might decide to dump my body down one of those abandoned mine shafts! Oh, God, I can't bear the thought of lying down in some awful hole with snakes, spiders, scorpions, and the rotting remains of other penniless—''

''All right, all right!'' Longarm shouted. ''I get the picture. For God sakes, Fishburn, don't fall apart right here in the street.''

''But what am I to do!''

Longarm knew that he couldn't leave this weak man unprotected. If he did and something bad befell him, Longarm would regret it the rest of his life. ''I'll escort you down to Silver City.''

Fishburn's sallow face lit up like a votive candle. ''Oh, Marshal, you will?''

"I said I would. And when I say something, I mean it."

"Thank you!" Fishburn reached for what Longarm supposed was his last few dollar bills.

"Keep your money."

"But I insist on paying you something!"

"Who knows? Someday I will need a good undertaker and perhaps you will be around."

"I hope not! I mean, in the sad event of your death, I'd prefer—"

"Never mind," Longarm said with mounting exasperation. "Let's just get started. I have business to attend to and not a lot of time to do it."

"You are extremely kind," Fishburn said. "At the very least, I'd like to write your superior and commend him for the fine work that you do."

"That ain't necessary. As a matter of fact, I've been sitting too much—first on a train, then today in the coach—and I could use a good hike down to Silver City and back up here. Get my blood pumping."

"I'm afraid that I am in rather poor condition and not accustomed to this elevation," the undertaker said, already sounding wheezy and out of breath. "But I promise that I'll do my very best."

Fortunately, it was less than a mile to The Divide. After that, it was all downhill to Silver City. There were a lot of men making the same hike up and down Gold Hill Canyon, and most of them were barrel-chested miners. As they walked, Longarm heard the tongues of many nationalities and saw that, if anything, mining activity had increased since his last visit.

They had to be careful not to be run down and trampled by the constant procession of huge ore wagons that carried rocks to the stamping mills that lined the Carson River some eight or ten miles to the south. Those ore wagons were pulled by oxen and mules, and the screeching protest of their wooden brakes was nearly intolerable.

The road was dry but rutted, and the ore wagons were constantly meeting oncoming traffic in the nature of supply and lumber wagons with fresh timbering for the deep Virginia City mines. Whenever these wagons met, there was a great amount of profanity and gamesmanship as the drivers vied for the right of way.

"Marshal Long, how do they all decide who will give way to whom?" Fishburn asked.

"The usual practice is for the uphill wagon to yield, but since they are so heavily burdened with ore and couldn't possibly back up, the lighter supply and timber wagons coming from downhill generally yield the right of way."

"I never heard such terrible cursing," Fishburn said, trying hard to keep up with Longarm as they passed the Gold Hill Hotel, where a couple of prostitutes were sitting on the balcony showing off their shapely ankles in the hopes of generating business. "Don't those drivers have a normal vocabulary that doesn't include the bad words?"

"Nope."

A few minutes more passed, and then Fishburn gasped, "I know this is totally outrageous, but if this Silver City position has already been filled, would you please lend me a couple of dollars and take me back up to the stage depot?"

Longarm had gotten too involved in this gentle soul's welfare to dump the hapless Fishburn in a place like Silver City, which, if anything, was even more wild and wicked than Virginia City. "Aw, I guess so."

"You are a *saint*!"

"No, I'm a sucker," Longarm groused.

Just then, a pair of drunken miners locked in combat crashed through the bat-wing doors of a saloon, reeled about in a couple of twisting revolutions, and then toppled into the street. They were short but powerful fellows, and they appeared to be intent on killing each other, for they were covered with blood and their shirts were torn to rags. Longarm started to move around them and continue on down the road, but Fishburn stopped and gaped.

"Marshal, one of them is going to kill the other! We can't let that happen, can we?"

"I haven't got time to interfere," Longarm snapped. "Brawls are commonplace up here, and I didn't see a weapon in either man's fist."

"But . . . but they're *really* hurting each other! Oh, my heavens, one is trying to gouge the other's eyeball out with his thumb! Marshal, please!"

Longarm stopped dead in his tracks and turned. Fishburn was telling the truth. "Aw, hell," he muttered, "maybe I better put a stop to this after all."

He drew his gun, which he carried on his left hip so that it came out in a cross-draw, then marched over to the pair of bloodied fighters and shouted, "United States Deputy Marshal! Stop fighting or I'll arrest you both!"

The two men paused for a moment and glanced up at

him. One of them spat out a bloody tooth and cursed. Then they went back to their brawling.

"Marshal, what are you going to do?"

Longarm pistol-whipped them both. He had done it so often that he knew exactly how hard to plant his barrel across a man's skull without doing permanent injury.

"Marshal!" Fishburn cried with horror. "I thought you were going to arrest them!"

"I was bluffing," Longarm snapped. "Dammit, I haven't got the time."

Fishburn was going to heighten his protest, but Longarm grabbed him by the collar and propelled him down the road.

"Is that it?" Longarm asked, pointing to a building beside which a black hearse was parked and on which a sign read: "B. T. CRUTCHFIELD, UNDERTAKER AND DENTIST.

"Yes, that's it. But I didn't know the man was a dentist!"

"Undertakers and barbers often double as dentists," Longarm explained. "I expect that you'll have to learn to pull a few bad teeth yourself."

"Never!"

"Get in there and ask for the job," Longarm said, fast losing patience.

Fishburn slapped the dust off his black coat and took a deep breath. "If he throws me out, you won't leave me down here, will you?"

"I'll give you five minutes," Longarm said, pulling out his pocket watch. "Five minutes to learn if you are gonna get hired or not. After that, I'm leaving. I've just got too damn much to do for any more screwing around with you, Fishburn.''

''Thank you!''

Longarm drew a cigar from his coat pocket and sat down on the building's front steps. He lit his cigar, and watched as some other drunken miners came out to drag their now-unconscious friends out of the dusty street before they were squashed by the steady and profane procession of ore and supply wagons.

After a few minutes, Longarm twisted around and, through the building's front window, observed Fishburn engaged in conversation with a large, bald man who was doing most of the talking.

''He ain't going to land the damn job,'' Longarm mumbled with disgust. ''He ain't fit for doing anything up here on the Comstock Lode, and it's going to cost me a couple of dollars just to get him back to Reno, then send him back over the Sierras to California. I don't know why I always let myself get talked into these things.''

Before the five minutes were up, Fishburn came flying out the front door. He struck one of the porch posts and collapsed in a daze.

''You scrawny, squeamish little bastard!'' the big bald undertaker shouted. ''How *dare* you suggest that I can't pull teeth and still be a professional undertaker!''

An instant later, the door slammed shut and Longarm heaved a sigh, then got up and dragged Fishburn's limp body over to a watering trough.

''Come on,'' he said, dunking the man's head in the water, ''wake up!''

Fishburn sputtered into consciousness, and Longarm

hailed a buckboard, knowing that the Californian would never make the strenuous hike back up and over The Divide and into Virginia City.

"Hey! I'm a United States Marshal and I need a ride up to Virginia City!"

"Him too?"

Longarm nodded. "Yeah."

"Two bits apiece and you ride in the wagon bed."

Longarm nodded. He picked Fishburn up, tossed him into the buckboard, then hopped up and paid the driver. At least, he thought, trying to be fair, Fishburn had had enough gumption to ask for a job and then voice his professional reservations.

Chapter 11

"All right," Longarm said as they approached the stage office, "I'll buy your fare back to Reno and loan you a couple of dollars so that you can return to Sacramento."

"I can't thank you enough, and I'll repay you just as soon as I get back on my feet."

Longarm believed the man was sincere in his intentions and that, someday, he might even see his money again. "Steven," he said, "I've been wondering why you became an undertaker."

"I've wondered about that myself more than once. I don't really like the profession, but my father was an undertaker and I learned from him. I wanted to be a schoolteacher, but that didn't work out."

"Why not?"

The slender young man looked away, and Longarm saw pain in his expression and heard some bitterness in his voice when he said, "The larger boys can be pretty cruel and unruly. I couldn't seem to control them, and they mocked and insulted me until I decided that I was unsuited for that profession."

"Maybe you should have—"

"What? Tried to physically discipline the bullies? No, thank you. I'm not a fighter, Marshal. I do some things well, but I was a failure at administering discipline or punishment."

"There are plenty more occupations that you might enjoy more than being an undertaker. It's not that we don't need them, but . . . well, you understand."

"Of course I do. I am not very much like my father, who passed out business cards saying, 'You stab them, I'll slab them.' "

Longarm had to struggle to keep a straight face. "That's what he said?"

"Sure, it was his motto. He always told me that you had to have a slightly strange sense of humor to be a good undertaker. I suspect he was right."

"But you don't have a 'strange sense of humor.' "

"No, I don't."

"Then you should find something else to do. What are your interests and talents?"

"I write poetry," Steven said, "but that doesn't pay. Poets starve and I'm already thin. I'm also a pretty good artist, but artists starve too."

"Some can make a fair living," Longarm replied, wanting to offer encouragement.

"I know, but not many. Actually, I have a number of pen-and-ink sketches. I can sketch most anything. Old buildings, landscapes, people, and animals. I have a few sketches that I made coming over from Sacramento in my valise."

"I'd like to see them sometime."

Steven snapped his fingers and reached to open his valise. "Perhaps I could offer you a few right now in exchange for the money I'm borrowing!"

"Steven, it's not that I wouldn't enjoy your sketches, but I'm always out on some job and wouldn't have time to appreciate them."

"Sure," Fishburn said, looking disappointed. "But they're pretty good. I've actually sold quite a few. None for a lot of money, but once I learned that people liked to have themselves done in a slightly flattering light, I could sit in a public place and do them all day long for two bits each."

"Maybe that's your calling. Miners have money up here, and I bet they'd pay a lot more than two bits to have you draw their portraits so they could send them back home to their families and sweethearts."

"You could be right. But I still don't think I'm suited for the Comstock Lode. I guess I'll go home to Sacramento."

"To work in your father's business?"

"Yeah. He said he'd take me back."

Longarm scowled. "It's none of my business, but it sounds to me like you are giving up way too easy. And sure, the Comstock Lode is a rough and wide-open mining town. But they also attract very famous actors and actresses, politicians and lecturers. Don't be too quick to judge everyone up here as crude, violent, and illiterate."

"I'm sure you are right, but I'm going back to California."

"That's your decision." Longarm consulted his watch. "Let's go inside and find out when the next stagecoach is leaving for Reno."

"Okay."

Longarm was on a first-name basis with everyone who worked for the stage line. "Howdy, Jeff," he called in greeting to the owner's son, a handsome kid of about sixteen who would eventually take over the business if the Comstock didn't go bust first.

"Marshal Long! How are you?"

"Fine. This is my friend Steven Fishburn. He needs a one-way ticket back to Reno this evening."

"I'm sorry, but we canceled today's evening run."

"Why?" Longarm pointed to a sign denoting the arrival and departure times from Reno. "It says that there is another run at six-thirty."

"I know," Jeff admitted, "but we had to make special arrangements on account of Miss Belcher comin' up and givin' a talk this evening at the Opera House. A lot of people from Reno are coming up tonight and staying until tomorrow. I'm sorry, Mr. Fishburn."

"Isn't there some other means of getting to Reno this evening?"

Jeff shrugged. "You could rent a horse, but that is very expensive because they'd have to bring him back up here to Virginia City."

"I'm not interested in renting a horse anyway," Steven said. "I don't like horses. Anyway, your sign says that your first coach leaves at eight o'clock tomorrow morning."

"Yes, sir, but that coach is already booked, and so are the rest of the runs up until four o'clock."

"Could I sleep overnight on one of your office benches?"

"Afraid our insurance won't allow that. I suppose that you could sleep out in our barn, but. . . ."

"Never mind," Longarm said with mounting exasperation. "Steven, I'll lend you a few more dollars for a decent room along with a good breakfast."

"You *are* a saint!"

"A sucker," Longarm repeated as he paid for Steven's ticket on the next day's four o'clock stage. "I'm going to need some cash and I'm hoping that there is fresh expense money waiting at the telegraph office."

"Then let's go find out," Steven said, carefully pocketing his ticket.

The telegraph office was just a block away, and Longarm felt better to learn that Billy Vail had wired him a full hundred dollars.

"All right," Longarm said, feeling flush, "let's get us a couple of rooms, and then I want to be back at the stage depot when Miss Belcher and Miss Howe arrive."

"Looks like a stage is coming up the street right now," Steven said.

"Damned if it isn't. And I'll bet it's carrying those two women."

When Katherine saw Longarm, she momentarily forgot that he had fallen out of Gertrude's favor and waved.

"Who is *that*?" Steven asked, staring as he removed his cheap hat.

"Here name is Miss Katherine Howe. She's Hatchet Belcher's assistant and cut from the same piece of cloth.

A suffragist and a teetotaler who has no tolerance for other people's right to drink and have fun."

"Drink is the cause of a lot of the world's evils and suffering," Steven said. "While I was growing up and seeing all the bodies brought in to my father's business, I learned very early on that alcohol was a demon."

Longarm made a face. "You ought to join up with that pair, Steven! All you have to do is to tell them that you share their belief that liquor is the devil's brew and they'll welcome you with open arms."

He grinned. "I wouldn't mind being in Miss Howe's open arms one darn bit! She's beautiful."

"So is a coral snake."

"Does she also carry a hatchet?"

"No, she carries a gun, and take it from me. Katherine knows how and when to use it."

"She has magnificent facial features and her hair is gorgeous."

Longarm watched as Steven pulled sketch paper and an ink pen from his valise, then began to rapidly draw the young woman's portrait as soon as Katherine was helped down from the coach.

"Damn, you *are* good!"

Steven didn't look up, but said, "I've been drawing all my life, but rarely have I seen anyone so beautiful as Miss Howe."

"Well," Longarm said, "she's pretty, all right. But you make her look even better."

"That would be impossible."

The sketch was not large, but it was full-bodied, and Longarm was very impressed. It was easy to believe that Steven could, had he wished, have made a very nice living simply by taking up residence in one of the more popular saloons and becoming a portrait artist. He would, of course, have to give the saloon a percentage, but he would still do extremely well, and the saloon would take good care of him and make certain that he was well treated and always paid for his work. Longarm decided to pass on this fine idea.

"Marshal, please excuse me," Steven said before Longarm could pass along his inspired suggestion.

He watched the young man hurry over toward the two suffragists, and then saw the Reno lawmen stop him in his tracks.

"He's all right," Longarm said, going to intervene.

"What the hell are *you* doing up here?" Marshal Horton demanded.

Before Longarm could answer, Gertrude said, "Yes, why *are* you up here?"

"Oh," Longarm said, determined to keep the conversation amicable, "I thought I'd just come along to make sure that your newfound protectors didn't mess up on the job."

"Really, Marshal Long. I don't wish to be associated with you any longer. There is already enough blood on your hands."

Longarm forgot about being amicable. "Miss Belcher, if you are referring to what happened between me and that Reno bouncer, I killed the man in self-defense and in front of many witnesses."

"Perhaps so, but it was a tragic affair that left a bad taste in my mouth. Marshal Horton assures me that all necessary precautions will be taken to insure that there is no more bloodshed."

"Miss Belcher, I don't want to alarm you, but no one can predict what will happen when you begin to voice your strong and highly unpopular stand on prohibition in a town where the saloons outnumber all other businesses combined."

Gertrude was about to respond when she happened to see Katherine and Steven. He was presenting her with the sketch that he had just completed, and it was easy to see by her expression that she was even more impressed than Longarm with the young man's artistic ability.

"Miss Howe," Steven said, face glowing with pleasure and admiration, "your face is too beautiful for even Rembrandt to paint. My effort is a poor reflection of your loveliness, but I offer it to you with my heartfelt admiration and devotion."

"Did you hear *that*," Marshal Horton said, looking at the young man from Sacramento as if he were some kind of idiot.

"I heard," Longarm answered. "He told me he wrote poetry, but I didn't give it much notice until now."

Gertrude marched over to the young couple, and although a passing wagon drowned out the conversation, Longarm could tell by looking at the older woman that she was being won over. She kept glancing at the sketch and then up at Steven. Soon, she was smiling just as widely as Katherine.

"Who is that skinny sonofabitch anyway?" Marshal Horton snarled.

"I thought I knew," Longarm said with newfound admiration. "Now, I'm not so sure."

"Is he your friend?"

"I guess you could say that."

"Why did you take up with the likes of him?"

"He needed some help, and besides, I kind of enjoy his company. Marshal, we can't all be off the same mold. Steven is a poet and and artist at heart, but right now he's sort of at loose ends. He needs a break."

Horton wasn't listening. "That scarecrow is so skinny a good breeze would knock him down."

"Yeah," Longarm said as much to himself as to Horton. "But he sure knows how to impress Eastern women."

"He don't impress me a damn bit! And I think I'll run him the hell off."

"Marshal," Longarm said, catching the man's sleeve. "Can I give you a little piece of advice?"

"I guess."

"If you run young Steven right now, those two women are going to run *you*. I suggest that you just let well enough alone."

"And I suggest you call that weasel in and tell him that these women are under my protection."

Longarm said nothing as the fool went over and interrupted the trio. A few moments later, Marshal Horton was standing red-faced in the dust while Steven and the suffragists headed for what would probably be a very sober but interesting supper.

Chapter 12

Forty-five minutes before Gertrude Belcher was to appear on stage at Piper's Opera House, Marshal Ben Horton said to his deputies, "I want everyone who comes here tonight to hand over their guns at the door. And I mean *everyone*."

"What about hideout guns?" Deputy Joe Cutter asked. "Are we supposed to frisk all the people or just take their six-shooters?"

"Just ask them to remove their side arms," Horton replied after a moment's deliberation. "It would be impossible to frisk everyone that will be coming through the door."

"There are back doors and side exits," Longarm said. "I've already instructed the manager to lock them so no one can sneak in with a six-gun or even a rifle that they could use from across the room."

"Those doors will have to be unlocked as soon as possible according to local fire laws," Horton told him. "If we get a couple hundred people here tonight and some prankster yells 'fire,' we don't want to have a stampede for the front door and have folks get trampled to death."

"The other exits can all be opened from the inside, but not the outside," Longarm said. "I've already checked them out."

"Marshal Long, is there anything else you want to say?" Horton asked. "Or can I begin to do *my* job?"

Longarm ignored the sarcasm. Moments earlier, he had hurried over from the Stratton House, where the two suffragists were guests at an elegant dinner attended by many local supporters as well as Dan De Quille, who would give the affair a good write-up in the *Territorial Enterprise*. Steven had also been invited to the exclusive meal, and from what Longarm had gathered, the young man from Sacramento had fit right in with that group and was being besieged with requests for personal sketches. Longarm just hoped that Steven wasn't doing them *all* for free so that he'd earn enough money tonight to repay his loan.

"All right," Horton was saying, "I couldn't get Miss Belcher to tell me exactly what she is going to say tonight, but we can expect it will be strong talk about the evils of liquor and the injustice of women still being denied the vote in most states and territories. That's what she talked about in Reno, and I doubt her pitch will be much different tonight."

"She wouldn't try and bust up any saloons tonight, would she?" Deputy Joe Cutter asked.

"I don't think so," Horton replied, looking over at Longarm for confirmation.

Longarm shrugged. "From what I have observed of Miss Belcher, we ought to be prepared for anything. The woman has no fear whatsoever, and I don't think even she knows what she will say. Let's just hope that she doesn't decide to go on a rampage with her damned hatchet."

"Have you actually seen the damned thing?" Horton asked.

Longarm dipped his chin in assent. "She carries it in that big black purse of hers and keeps it sharp."

"That's all we need," Cutter groused. "If she goes rampaging down C Street, there will be a riot."

"That's right," the other deputy, whose name was Doug Potter, agreed. "They'll lynch her for certain, and I doubt that there's a damn thing we could do to stop 'em."

"Potter, if that's your attitude, you might as well take a walk," Longarm told the man.

Potter's eyes dropped to the floor and he said, "Aw, I didn't really mean it."

"I hope not," Longarm grated.

"Leave him alone," Horton ordered. "He works for me, not you."

"That's true," Longarm said, "but I don't work with people that I can't count on when the going gets tough."

"You can count on Doug," Deputy Cutter said. "He and I have been in a few fixes and he ain't backed down yet."

"All right, then. Who's going over to get the women and escort them over here?"

''I'll take care of that,'' Horton offered. ''And I'll take my deputies.''

''Good. I'll stay here by the door and make sure that no one tries to sneak in early.''

The next hour was hectic. The crowd began to arrive well before the suffragists, and Longarm didn't make any friends when he insisted that everyone leave their guns at the door.

''Damn foolishness!'' a man grumbled. ''We came to *support* those ladies, not shoot them!''

''I'm sure that you did,'' Longarm said. ''But there have been several attempts on their lives in just the short time I've been with Miss Belcher and Miss Howe.''

When this news filtered through the crowd, it became less resentful. Soon, Marshal Howe appeared with the two women close behind and his deputies behind *them,* their hands close to their guns, their eyes scanning the audience.

''Big crowd,'' Horton said as Gertrude and Katherine passed into the cavernous opera house. ''Must be three hundred people here tonight. I'm impressed.''

''There are at least *five* hundred,'' Gertrude snapped as the audience saw her, then rose to its feet giving the famous woman a standing ovation.

The two women marched up to the stage, and Longarm noted that Steven Fishburn and Dan De Quille had been given center seats in the front row. Then, without preamble, Gertrude Hatchet Belcher began her tirade against demon liquor.

''Ladies and gentlemen, I have personally suffered the degradation that comes with living among drunks! My father was a drunk. My brothers became drunks, and . . . had I been born a man, I most likely would have become a drunk right along with them!"

The audience sat riveted with attention. From opposite sides of the house, two women began to sob. Gertrude's expression turned dark, and she reminded Longarm of a mother studying her children with intense disapproval. She extended her arm very slowly, pointing a finger at everyone.

"My friends, you and I all know that Satan created liquor to destroy the godliness in this world. Who can imagine the heartache and the degradation that liquor has caused! Is there *anyone* among you who has not seen families torn asunder by demon liquor? Or wives beaten senseless by drunken husbands? Or husbands laid low and then destroyed by this liquid poison? If even one of you can say that liquor has not been the bane of humanity, then stand up!"

No one stood. Gertrude studied them with the burning eyes of an evangelist. She was in complete control of the audience, which seemed to hold its breath.

Even Longarm was captured by her dynamic presence, but he had heard the speech before, and so was able to divert his attention toward the hushed crowd. He searched for any sign of a fanatic who might be reaching for a deadly hideout gun. Or perhaps someone up in the first row with a throwing knife. There were men who had the skill to throw knives with both speed and accuracy. Longarm had once been a knife-thrower's target. Only instinct and luck had prevented him from being skewered.

Gertrude's voice rolled over the audience like the

voice of an angry god. "My friends, when is this nation going to face the fact that liquor is the single greatest curse on our society! That it robs men of their spirit and their divinity! That it *destroys* . . ."

Marshal Horton came over to Longarm and whispered, "I sure wish that she wouldn't whip them up like this. To tell you the truth, though, it almost makes me want to give up drinkin' nothing but milk and water."

"Not me," Longarm replied, feeling the tension build higher and higher. "Let's just keep our eyes open and our mouths shut. Okay?"

Horton's face colored with anger and he moved away. Longarm knew he'd angered the Reno marshal, but he didn't care. Horton was getting too damn talky anyway.

Gertrude Belcher had a habit of weaving in both of her passionate issues, and now she introduced the subject of a woman's right to vote. "We all know that the great President and martyr Abraham Lincoln freed the slaves, and it cost him his life and America untold heartache and carnage. But it was the *right and moral* thing to do! Isn't that so!"

The audience shook the very rafters of the opera house when it cried, "Yes!"

Gertrude finally relaxed, and even gave her listeners a smile. Now she turned to Katherine Howe, who arose from her chair and came forward in a long white dress. She seemed almost angelic, and yet, as she took her place beside her mentor, she also spoke with an evangelist's passionate and ringing conviction.

"My name is Miss Katherine Howe," she began, "and I am twenty-three years old but do not have the rights of a freed slave in the state where I live. I have no say about how my country is to make its most important decisions. I have no voice! I am *nothing* in America's political process. Politicians do not seek my views nor do they care about the injustices I—and you—suffer!''

Katherine's voice trembled with righteous indignation and unimaginable sorrow. ''My friends, it is long, long past the time for states and territories to *give us our Constitutional right to vote*!''

At this ringing and powerful declaration, hundreds of women and men sprang to their feet and began to applaud like crazy. More than a few women even whistled like mule skinners, and Longarm realized that he was clapping his hands. And why not? Women everywhere deserved to vote! And if these two firebrands could only stick to that message and forget that silliness about ''demon liquor,'' Longarm would have supported them one hundred percent.

Katherine raised her arms and motioned the enthusiastic audience to sit down and let her continue, but they kept shouting their support.

Suddenly, Deputy Potter was charging up the aisle and then jumping up onto the stage in a mad dash to reach Katherine. In that same moment, Longarm also began to run for the stage and his hand streaked for his six-gun, although he could not as yet identify a target.

''Don't shoot!'' Longarm bellowed, suddenly realizing that Potter was so rattled that he was about to fire right down into the crowd.

Suddenly gunfire exploded from the first section of seats. Deputy Potter took a slug in the forehead and crashed over backward.

Longarm thought he saw the assassin in the audience, but had no clear shot as the audience panicked. More shots followed, and the crowd became hysterical as they stampeded for the exits. It was a nightmare. Up on the stage, Gertrude drew out her hatchet as the assassin shot at her, putting a slug in her arm and causing her to drop the famous hatchet. Katherine screamed as she was struck by a wild bullet and sent sprawling. Steven vaulted up onto the stage, grabbed her, and attempted to shield her from further injury.

Longarm had no chance for a safe shot, but now he did identify the assassin, who had just pitched a gun under the seats and then joined the stampede. The killer was handsome and well dressed. Longarm had no choice but to knock several spectators aside as his long legs allowed him to close the distance and then drag the assassin down. They struggled on the floor, and the assassin was strong and desperate to escape. He had a spring-loaded derringer up his sleeve, and almost managed to get it into his hand and fire a bullet before Longarm smashed his nose to pulp.

''Oh, no, you don't!'' Longarm gritted out, delivering a series of short but devastating blows to his face. Longarm kept punching until the blood flowed and the assassin lost consciousness and went limp.

''Let me handcuff him!'' Marshal Ben Horton cried. ''Get off of him!''

Longarm was glad to obey. He climbed to his feet and crawled up on the stage, where Gertrude and Steven were huddled protectively over Katherine, now lying in a pool of blood.

''Is she dead?'' Longarm shouted.

"She needs a doctor!" Steven cried. "She needs a doctor!"

There was little question about that. It only took a moment for Longarm to observe that a bullet had entered Katherine, then passed through her body to exit just above the hip.

Longarm tore open the back of Katherine's dress. He gritted his teeth when he saw that the assassin's bullet might actually have clipped Katherine's spine. She was bleeding profusely, and Longarm knew that the first thing to do was to stop the hemorrhaging or the young woman would die.

"What can I do, Marshal Long?" Steven cried. "What can I do for her?"

"Do you have a clean handkerchief?"

Steven jammed one into Longarm's hand, shouting, "Is she going to make it?"

"Maybe."

Longarm used the handkerchief to plug up the hole where the bullet had exited. The handkerchief filled with blood.

"Steven, find a doctor!"

The young man disappeared, and Longarm could hear him yelling and shouting. Gertrude was calm but very pale. Her arm was bleeding, but Longarm could see at a glance that the wound was superficial.

"Dammit, Marshal Long, I should *never* have come here!" the suffragist cried.

Longarm ignored the outburst. "Miss Belcher, she's still bleeding heavily, but I think this girl has a fighting chance. What have you got that I can use to help stop the bleeding?"

Gertrude tore off a long woolen scarf, shouting, "Let's wrap this tight around her and see if that works!"

"Good idea."

The scarf did what they hoped, and a few moments later a doctor finally arrived. It took only a moment for him to determine that Deputy Potter was beyond help. Then, he hurried over to Katherine and made a quick examination that ended when he said, "We need to strap her on a litter and get her to my surgery."

Tears began to flow down Gertrude's plump cheeks. "Doctor, will she be paralyzed?"

"Dammit, she may not even live! We must hurry!"

Two days later, Dr. Charles Nelson announced, "Miss Howe is very weak and still drifting in and out of consciousness, but there is no doubt that she will make a full recovery and I detect absolutely no spinal damage."

Gertrude wept with joy, and so did Steven Fishburn. Longarm felt as if a ton of bricks had slipped from his shoulders. However, this welcome news was certainly no cause for celebration. Deputy Doug Potter had died almost instantly, and there were a lot of grievous injuries suffered during the stampede to exit Piper's Opera House. Even more depressing was the fact that the man they had captured had refused to talk, and then had been shot to death through the cell window that faced the alley. Marshal Ben Horton had not considered it necessary to post a twenty-four-hour guard outside the jail cell window.

To Longarm's way of thinking, the entire affair had been disastrous, and it all could have been avoided if Gertrude had listened to reason and stayed away from the Comstock Lode.

"Don't blame her," Steven said that evening. "The woman feels bad enough."

"I'm sure that she does," Longarm said. "And I support her crusade to win the vote, but the Comstock Lode is the wrong place to preach her message, especially that of prohibition. There are just too damn many drunks and lunatics up here. I predicted what happened at Piper's Opera House, but she wouldn't listen!"

"Was the assassin working alone?"

"We have no idea. No one seems to be able to identify our prisoner. He was a stranger, and that tells me he was probably a hired gunman rather than an individual who hated the idea of prohibition or stood to lose heavily from its enactment.

"Hell, Steven, we don't even know who killed him. It could have been someone bent on revenge, or it could even have been someone who hired the man! That's the thing that is driving me crazy. We haven't any leads. Nothing!"

"Marshal Horton is trying to talk Gertrude into leaving for Reno, but she won't go without Katherine," Fishburn said. "She also believes that gunman was part of a conspiracy paid for by the local saloon owners."

"That is not beyond the realm of possibility," Longarm growled.

"Yeah, but Gertrude confided that she intends to get out her hatchet and bust up a couple of saloons."

Longarm shook his head. "That's the *last* thing that she ought to do up here! Steven, the woman appears to like you. Talk some sense into her. Tell her to get off the Comstock Lode and go back where she came from before anyone else is killed."

"She won't go without Miss Howe."

"It will be weeks before Katherine can travel."

"The doctor says it will take months. Marshal, will you stay up here until they can travel?"

Longarm had also been giving that question some hard thought. And as much as he hated to, he said, "I have no choice but to stay and try to keep them from any further harm. My orders were to stay with those women until they were on their way back to the East."

"At least it will give you time to do an investigation."

"Yeah," Longarm said. "And I'll find out what is behind the assassination attempt even if I have to interview every sonofabitch on the Comstock Lode."

"If it begins to look like a conspiracy," Steven told him, "I'd like to know."

"Why?"

"If it was, I'd like to help."

Longarm understood. Steven Fishburn had not left Katherine for more than a few minutes since she'd been shot. The young man from Sacramento was deeply in love with the wounded suffragist.

"When this is over," Longarm asked, "how are you going to pick up your life in Sacramento?"

"I'm not going back. I'm . . . well, I'm staying here as long as Katherine needs me. I'm making friends and I've been asked to do a lot of sketches. Marshal, I think that I can make a lot of money drawing up here and still have plenty free time to care for Katherine."

"Well," Longarm said as he prepared to send Billy Vail a telegram that his boss in Denver sure wasn't going to appreciate, "they say that every cloud has a silver lining."

"Katherine doesn't think I should be an undertaker either."

"Well," Longarm said, pausing at the door and dredging up a smile, "I guess that makes it unanimous."

Chapter 13

Longarm's telegram to Billy Vail in Denver was short and to the point:

> ASSASSINATION ATTEMPT ON SUFFRAGISTS APPEARS TO BE A CONSPIRACY RATHER THAN AN INDIVIDUAL ACT. **STOP** IF TRUE OTHER ASSASSINATION ATTEMPTS LIKELY **STOP** WILL REMAIN ON COMSTOCK UNTIL SITUATION RESOLVED UNLESS ORDERED OTHERWISE **STOP**

"You really think that opera house shootin' a couple nights back was organized and not just the work of one fella?" the telegraph operator whispered so that no one else could overhear him.

"That's right, but don't you dare breathe a word about it to anyone or you'll be breaking a federal law."

"Hell," the telegraph operator, an old man with a flowing white mustache, snorted, "do you think I don't know that? I never tell anyone anything! I've heard secrets that would make even an old Irish priest's ears burn, but I never batted an eye nor whispered a word."

"Look, old-timer, I didn't mean to insult you but this is damned important."

"Sure it is! If there's killers workin' to do in them Eastern women, they're gonna be interested in your plans."

"That's right. In fact," Longarm said, "I imagine they might even be watching me right now."

The telegraph operator blinked, then surveyed the street outside. "Well," he finally concluded, "they can watch me until Hell freezes over, but I ain't gonna tell 'em anything. If I did, I would deserve to lose my job."

"Send the telegram."

The telegram was sent, and Longarm immediately destroyed the paper he'd written it out upon. "I expect that I'll be receiving an answer within the hour, so I'll be back."

"I'll be here until closin' time," the old man said. "If it comes in, I'll have your answer ready."

"Thanks."

Longarm went to the offices of the *Territorial Enterprise* and asked to see his old friend Dan De Quille. The tall, somewhat cadaverous-looking man was hunched over a desk writing when Longarm was escorted into the cluttered editorial offices. Dan looked up and said, "Custis, how is Miss Katherine Howe feeling today?"

"Much better. You got a minute to talk in private?"

"Sure. Let's step into my outer office."

Dan unfolded from the chair and headed out the back door into an open alleyway where he liked to smoke and did some of his best interviews.

In his mid-fifties, the man was painfully thin, and Longarm knew that he was restless and didn't take proper care of himself as he prowled the Comstock for its most unusual stories. De Quille was an institution in Virginia City, and nearly everyone liked and trusted him. Unfortunately, they often fed his excessive love of liquor with free drinks in exchange for a little local gossip or a humorous Comstock tale of the kind that Dan could spin for hours over a bar. The stories of De Quille out on the town celebrating were legendary, and when he became very drunk, he would reminisce about his escapades with the now-famous Mark Twain.

"What's on your mind?" Dan asked without preliminaries.

Custis came right to the point. "I'm beginning to think that the opera house shooting was the work of conspirators."

De Quille's bushy eyebrows lifted. "Oh? What makes you think so?"

"I don't think that fella that was shot to death in his jail cell was just some lunatic or fanatic."

"Then who was he?"

"My guess is that he was a professional killer, and that means that I need to find out who is behind the assassination attempt on Miss Belcher and Miss Howe."

"What gives you the idea that the man was a professional? And why would any professional be foolish enough to attempt murder in an audience full of Miss Belcher's supporters?"

"Money. If you pay enough money, you can always find someone willing to take even the greatest risk. Besides, think about the circumstances surrounding the assassination attempt. Remember that we had removed everyone's side arms so there was just myself, Ben Horton, and his two deputies who were supposed to be armed."

" 'Supposed to be armed' is the key phrase here," De Quille said. "A determined man can always find a way to conceal a weapon unless he is thoroughly searched."

"I know that. What is the point?"

"The point is that when the shooting started, I dived under the seats like a lot of other people. But I saw the killer and he looked like a fanatic to me. So, unless you have some evidence to support your theory, I can't believe that he wasn't just a madman who must have had some bizarre and murderous motive that we will probably never understand."

"If that were the case, why was he gunned down in his cell the first night we had him in custody?"

De Quille frowned, and then waved his hand in a gesture of indifference. "I suspect he was shot by another lunatic, only this one had the opposite view and was sympathetic to the issues of women's suffrage and prohibition."

"Dan, the man that opened fire in Piper's Opera House *was* a professional. He had a hideout gun up his sleeve, and he would probably have shot me to death if I hadn't been fortunate enough to accidentally grab his forearm and disrupt the spring-loaded mechanism."

But De Quille still wasn't convinced, or perhaps he just wanted to push Longarm's reasoning to the limit.

"Custis," he said, "there are a lot of cardsharps who have those spring-loaded devices, and most of them deliver hole cards, but they also can be adapted to a derringer. So it *could* have been a professional *cardsharp* who went crazy."

"But what if my hunch is right and the killer was paid to assassinate Miss Belcher and Miss Howe?"

"Then we do have a big, big problem."

"Can we in good conscience ignore that possibility?"

De Quille plucked a cigar from Longarm's vest pocket. He lit it and inhaled, then said, "No, we cannot."

"Then we need to start looking for the conspirators," Longarm said. "And that's why I've come for your help. You know everyone who is anyone on the Comstock Lode."

"That's true."

"And I think we can safely assume that whoever might have paid and then shot their hired gun has guts and money. We're not looking for some hardworking miner."

"True again," De Quille said, examining the cigar he'd taken from Longarm. "Good God, can't you afford any better cigar than this?"

"Not when I have friends like you that are always bumming them off me for nothing."

"What *exactly* do you want me to do?"

"I wish I could say," Longarm replied. "I suppose I would like you to just start digging up some dirt. I understand that you have paid informants who are privy to everything of importance that occurs on the Comstock."

"Yes, but mostly in regard to what is happening way

down in the biggest mines. And even that information can be highly dangerous if given to the wrong people who stand to win or lose from buying or selling mining stock."

"Besides the saloons, who stands to lose the most if prohibition were to become the law of the land?"

"The American drinking man. People like myself."

"Who else?"

"The breweries and distilleries, of which we have at least seven. Liquor wholesalers and the freighters and their companies who bring it in, mostly from California. There are dozens of those outfits because the Comstock Lode has a raging thirst."

"Then those are the people we should be looking at," Longarm told him.

"Custis, you ask a great deal but offer very little other than the possibility of being murdered for meddling."

"Are you asking for money?"

"Of course not!" De Quille looked very offended. "I just want you to be fully aware that I do value my life, as dissipated as it might outwardly appear."

"I know a man who will give you a good burial. He owes me and will do it for free."

De Quille chuckled and drew a silver flask from his pocket. He uncapped the flask and took several long swallows, then sighed and wiped his lips. He extended the flask to Longarm, who also took a pull.

"Ahh!" Longarm gasped. "Dan, can't you even afford good whiskey?"

"Not in the quantities that I require," De Quille said without shame or hesitation. "And now that our business is finished, why don't you invite me out to dinner?"

"Because I am probably being watched. Therefore, it might not be wise to appear together in public."

"Excellent point!" De Quille extended his bony hand, and when Longarm took it he said, "I promise you that I will put my ear to the ground, so to speak, and let a few of my most trusted lieutenants know that I want to learn if there is some plot or conspiracy to murder either Miss Belcher or Miss Howe."

"Thank you."

"Do you think that Miss Belcher will bring out her famous hatchet and take to our saloons?"

"I hope not," Longarm replied. "I think that this last attack has actually unnerved her into becoming a little more reasonable."

"I hope you are wrong," De Quille said, "because if Miss Belcher goes on the attack with that famous hatchet of hers, I could have a wonderful time lambasting her in our paper."

"Look beyond your own amusements," Longarm suggested. "Think of Miss Belcher's safety."

"You are right," De Quille admitted. "The woman would be shot, drawn, and quartered if she attempted to go on a rampage with her little hatchet. I wish neither her nor Miss Howe any more misfortune."

"Glad to hear that."

"That young man from Sacramento seems quite taken with Miss Howe."

"Yes, he is."

De Quille smiled mischievously. "Do we have a budding romance going on that might amuse my readers?"

"Let that gossip be," Longarm said. "Steven is a fine young man who is doing his best to change his attitude about life in general and the Comstock Lode in particular.''

''He does seem admirable. We have agreed to have supper together when we can find a mutually agreeable time.''

''Help him out if you can,'' Longarm urged. ''In addition to his talent as an artist, he also writes poetry. Maybe you can publish a few of his poems and sketches in your paper.''

''That thought has already occurred to me and is a real possibility. Do you think he might also be interested in journalism?''

''I think so.''

De Quille finished his cigar and then announced, ''I will let you know the moment I hear anything of interest concerning the possibility of conspirators.''

''Thanks.''

Longarm left the newspaperman and found his way back to the telegraph operator's office by way of the alley. He was feeling somewhat better now because, if there was a conspiracy, there was no more able person to uncover it than Dan De Quille.

The telegraph office was closed. Longarm consulted his watch. That was odd. It was still way too early for the old codger to have closed up for the day.

He knocked on the door and tried to peek through the window, but the office appeared empty. Going back to the door, he tested the knob and discovered it to be unlocked. Longarm went inside, and that was when he saw the operator's body lying slumped beside his desk.

Longarm drew his six-gun and crouched low. He looked all around, but the office was silent and abandoned. He checked the operator's pulse. There was none.

"Damn," Longarm swore in anger and frustration as he searched without success for an incoming telegram from Denver. "I think I just got this poor old man killed!"

Chapter 14

Each day, Longarm met with Dan De Quille in a secret place where they would not be observed, but the newspaperman could not reveal any news of a conspiracy behind the attack on Gertrude and Katherine.

"Custis, whoever is behind this—if there *is* anyone behind it—is being very secretive. None of my informants has heard anything that would indicate a conspiracy."

This was not what Longarm wanted to hear. "Dan, of course there is a conspiracy! What other reason could there be for the murder of the telegraph operator? *Someone* must know who gunned that old man down as well as our jailed prisoner."

"The rumors are that the opera house gunman was an outsider. Most likely, he arrived in town the very day that he opened fire at Piper's Opera House. I'm working on that, and it looks like he might have come from Arizona."

"That supports my theory that the man wasn't acting on his own out of hatred or fanaticism. If he had just arrived that day, then he must have been a hired gunman. Someone who had to believe that he could kill Miss Belcher and probably Miss Howe as well and then use the pandemonium to make good his escape."

"I have some other news, Custis, but you're not going to like hearing it."

"Tell me."

"The word is that Miss Belcher isn't as unnerved as we thought by the opera house shooting and intends to go breaking up saloons in the very near future."

Longarm groaned. "That's all we need. I had better speak to her."

"She'll deny those intentions," De Quille predicted. "She'll have to because you might try to stop her."

"Has Marshal Horton heard this rumor?"

"I have no idea," De Quille admitted. "But it wouldn't surprise me. Hatchet Belcher didn't become famous by giving speeches. She's famous because of her hatchet-wielding rampages."

"I was hoping that this latest brush with death might have caused her to change her tactics," Longarm said, "but I guess it didn't. Thanks for the warning."

"You had better talk that woman out of her plans," the newspaperman warned, "or there will be hell to pay."

"I know."

Longarm went to see Marshal Ben Horton, and was shocked to discover the Reno lawman getting drunk in the Silver Dollar Saloon. Horton was in no condition to protect anyone, even himself.

"Ben, what the hell is going on?"

"Me and Deputy Cutter are pulling stakes and going back to Reno to attend the funeral of Deputy Potter. We're just waitin' for the next stage. Wanna drink?"

"No."

"Your choice."

"Ben," Longarm said, choosing his words carefully in order not to antagonize the man, "I can appreciate you wanting to attend your deputy's funeral, but all along you have insisted on taking care of the suffragists until they returned to the East."

"Piss on 'em!" Horton spat as if he had bitten into a lemon. "I'm sorry as hell that I ever saw them two troublemakers! I remember that you also wanted to be in charge of their safety. Fine! United States Deputy Marshal Long, them two female snakes are all yours!"

"Thanks."

"Don't mention it. And if you somehow manage to get them off the Comstock Lode alive, then don't you dare let 'em put up in Reno for even one damned night! If I see 'em, I'll arrest 'em and throw away the key."

"On what charges?"

Hogan poured himself another whiskey. His eyes were bloodshot and his face was twisted with hatred. "What charges? Gawdammit, I'll charge 'em with being a public menace. Because of those two, good people are getting killed! I don't give a damn about that bastard that was plugged in his jail cell, but Deputy Potter was a *good* man! He left a wife and two small children, and I hold myself responsible for his death."

''Getting drunk isn't going to make things better,'' Longarm said. ''Why don't you—''

Horton took a swing at Longarm. He was so drunk and filled with self-loathing that he probably wanted Longarm to beat the hell of him. Maybe that would have made him feel a little better, but Longarm wasn't about to be a part of that game. So he just blocked the punch and then yanked Horton's arm up behind his back until the man grunted with pain and raised up on his toes.

''Break my arm, you big bastard!'' Horton gritted out. ''Go ahead!''

''Sorry,'' Longarm said, propelling the man out the saloon door and onto the sidewalk. ''Whether you care or not, you *are* a lawman and you swore to uphold the law. You're going to sober up and see things a little different. When that happens, maybe you won't judge yourself so hard.''

''Let go of me!''

''I'm taking you to the stage depot. If necessary, I'll hogtie and throw you on board so you have no choice but to behave. Where's Deputy Cutter?''

''He's already waitin' at the stage.'' Horton struggled, but Longarm had him firmly under control, and finally the man grated out, ''All right, Custis, let loose of me and I'll behave.''

''You sure?''

''I give you my word,'' Horton answered. ''At least that's still worth something.''

Longarm released the guilt-ridden lawman and stepped back with his fists raised. Hogan swayed precariously on his boot heels, and then turned and walked away.

Longarm watched the man until he disappeared. He had a feeling that Ben Horton's lawman days were over. Once a man got down on himself that bad, it was nearly impossible for him to do his job. Maybe Deputy Cutter would replace him.

"Marshal Long?"

Longarm turned to see a stranger. "What do you want?"

"I thought you'd like to know that Hatchet Belcher just went into the Bucket of Blood Saloon."

"And?"

"And she had her hatchet in her hand. I expect you're going to hear all hell breaking loose in about two seconds."

The stranger was right. Longarm heard Belcher scream like a puma, and then heard shouts and curses as men piled out of the busiest saloon in Virginia City as if being chased by Satan.

Longarm bolted into a run, but didn't make it halfway across C Street when he heard splintering wood. Drawing his own weapon, he slammed through the bat-wing doors of the saloon and skidded to an abrupt halt. Gertrude Belcher was stretched out on the sawdust floor with her infamous hatchet still clutched in her hand. She'd managed to cave in a cask of whiskey and a barrel of beer before someone had knocked her out cold.

"I hope she's dead," a pale-looking bartender hissed. "That woman is insane!"

"Who hit her?" Longarm asked.

"I did," a big miner with a bloody forearm said as he advanced a step to separate him from the still-gaping saloon crowd. "The woman was swinging that ax around, and she cut me on the arm when I tried to take it away.''

"How bad are you hurt?''

The miner shrugged and pulled up his sleeve, wiggling his fingers. "Not too bad. Looks worse than it feels.''

"So what did you hit her with?''

"My fist. I admit it, Marshal. I punched her in the head. I never slugged no woman before, but I'm glad that I slugged her. She's crazy!''

The bartender cleared his throat. "Marshal, are you gonna arrest her for destroying private property? She's cost this saloon big money.''

"How much?''

The bartender's eyes flicked to the leaking casket of whiskey and barrel of beer. "Be at least twenty dollars. It ain't cheap to bring liquor all the way from California.''

"Plug up the leaks and save what you can. As for the loss, here's twenty dollars.''

"You're payin'?''

"That's right.''

"What about my arm?'' the miner demanded. "I'm gonna need to get it sewed up and then replace this new woolen shirt!''

"All right,'' Longarm said, "here's ten dollars. That ought to more than pay for your shirt and the doctor.''

Longarm gently slapped the woman's cheeks, but she was out cold and there was little that he could do to rouse her.

"You *are* going to arrest her, aren't you, Marshal?'' the bartender asked again.

"I'll take care to see that she causes no more trouble on the Comstock Lode," Longarm promised as he scooped the unconscious woman up in his arms and carried her out the front door.

"What about this hatchet!" the bartender shouted as he rushed outside waving the famous instrument of destruction.

Longarm halted on the sidewalk, turned, and replied, "Tack it up on the wall for your customers to gawk at. It ought to draw a crowd."

"We'll do it!" the bartender cried, waving the hatchet and then dashing back inside the Bucket of Blood Saloon.

Longarm knew that he ought to take Gertrude Belcher over to the doctor's office for an examination, but he also knew that he'd just given his promise that she would cause no more trouble in Virginia City. That being the case, he carried Gertrude all the way over to the stage depot.

When he approached the stage, he said, "Driver, you have another passenger."

"Put her on board," the driver said with a wink. "I'll have this stage rockin' like a cradle, and with luck, that wildcat might sleep all the way down to Reno."

"I'll be gawdamned if I'll ride in the same coach with her!" Ben Horton snarled as he poked his head out the door.

"Then I suggest you climb up on the roof and tie yourself down so you don't fall off," Longarm told the man. "Because there will never be a better time to get Miss Belcher out of Virginia City than right now."

A minute later, it was done. Gertrude Belcher was

leaving the Comstock Lode. Maybe she'd return, but Longarm doubted it. Most likely, she'd go back East, regroup from this disastrous Western campaign, and then buy another hatchet. Longarm simply did not care. He was certain that Billy Vail and the politicians in Denver weren't going to be very happy with this ignoble outcome, but to hell with them. Too many men had died and the stakes were too high to play this game any longer. Besides, Longarm had more important business, and that was to find out who had hired the assassin. Trouble was, with Miss Belcher out of the picture, getting to the bottom of that mystery was going to be even harder.

Word of what had happened to Hatchet Belcher spread rapidly across the Comstock Lode. It spread so fast that when Longarm trudged back up C Street, miners piled out of the saloons and cheered him lustily. It was, Longarm thought, all a bit embarrassing.

Dan De Quille overtook him as he headed for his hotel room. "I want the particulars of the historic event," the newspaperman cried, matching Longarm stride for stride. "I want every last detail!"

"Why?" Longarm asked. "So you can lampoon the woman?"

"Among other things."

"I won't be a part of that," Longarm told the newspaperman. "Gertrude Belcher might have used the wrong tactics to get her message across, but her intentions were good."

"Are you saying that you are for prohibition?" De Quille asked with astonishment.

"No! I'm just saying that liquor does cause a lot of suffering and death."

"And a lot of laughter! My gawd, Custis, you know how brutal it is up here! What do you think these men would do if they didn't have strong drink to drown their miseries?"

"I don't know," Longarm replied. "Maybe they'd save their money and then go home to their families older, wiser, and richer."

"You've been around that fanatical woman far too long," De Quille said, looking worried. "Come on into the Bucket of Blood and show me exactly where Miss Belcher was laid out cold. I'll buy us a bottle of rye whiskey and we can put this entire matter into the proper perspective."

Longarm realized he really had nothing better to do. He still had no leads on any conspiracy. Miss Belcher, the great thorn in his side these past weeks, was gone and, he hoped, would soon be forgotten. So what reason was there not to join De Quille over a bottle and relax?

Unable to think of a legitimate reason, Longarm said, "All right, Dan. But I still mean to prove that someone hired that opera house gunman. And when I find them, they will be charged with the murder of Deputy Potter."

"Fair enough. I'll keep trying to find out whatever I can, and we can both ask around a little more freely now that Hatchet Belcher is out of the picture. But what about her young friend, Miss Howe?"

"What about her?" Longarm asked. "She's still recuperating and under the doctor's strict care."

"Do you think that *her* life is yet in danger?"

"I don't know," Longarm replied. "The fact of the matter is, I'm not too sure of anything right now except that drinking some whiskey sounds good."

"We'll have the best," De Quille promised, licking his thin lips. "I drink the best and so will you. Then, you will relate the fracas in great detail."

"I only arrived *after* Miss Belcher was unconscious. You'll have to ask the bartender and the other customers who were there to provide the details."

"I will!" De Quille proclaimed at the top of his voice. "You can be very sure that I will!"

Longarm suspected that the newspaperman had already been drinking a fair share of rye whiskey. To hell with it all anyway! For the first time in weeks, he was also going to get drunk.

Chapter 15

Longarm was moving slow the next morning, and he was quite sure that Dan De Quille was moving even slower. The previous evening, they'd drunk and talked until long after midnight. Dan had bought the first bottle of whiskey, and it had been as smooth as a baby's behind. After that was consumed, they'd been toasted and treated by the miners until they could drink no more. Everyone in the Bucket of Blood Saloon had seemed happy and relieved that Miss Belcher had left the Comstock Lode, most likely never to return. Now, it was time for breakfast.

"Coffee, flapjacks, potatoes, steak, and eggs," Longarm told the man when he arrived at the Owl Hoot Cafe. "And lots of everything."

"Normally, that would cost you two dollars, Marshal. But seeing as how you're the man that threw Hatchet

Belcher on the stage yesterday, it's on the house."

"Much obliged."

The coffee was strong and the food was tasty and plentiful. It was well after nine o'clock when Longarm strolled out of the cafe feeling like a new man. He exchanged greetings with several passersby, and then he went up the street to the telegraph office. It made him feel bad that there was a young man in the place of the old one who'd been murdered, and that reminded him that he could not leave this town until he also found out who was behind that man's death.

Whoever killed him knows that I am determined to stay until I get to the bottom of this, Longarm thought as he entered the office and began to write out another telegram to be sent to Billy Vail.

The new operator read the message and his hands were shaking. Wanting to reassure the young man, Longarm said, "Don't worry. I'll stay right here and wait until I get a response."

"Do you really thing old Jess was murdered because of . . . you know, that message that was sent back to you?"

"I'm afraid so," Longarm replied. "However, since my first telegram concerned Miss Belcher and she is no longer in Virginia City, I can't imagine that you are in any danger."

"But can you be *real* sure?"

"Nothing in life is sure," Longarm told the worried man. "But I'm staying here until I get a response, so there is nothing to worry about. Go ahead and send this telegram."

"Yes, sir."

MISS BELCHER NOW IN RENO AND EXPECTED TO RETURN EAST **STOP** AM STAYING IN VIRGINIA CITY UNTIL BUSINESS IS FINISHED AND MISS HOWE FEELS WELL ENOUGH TO ALSO RETURN EAST **STOP** MYSTERIOUS DEATHS UNDER INVESTIGATION **STOP** WILL KEEP YOU POSTED **STOP**

"I'll be glad when Miss Howe has made a recovery and is gone," the new telegraph operator said in an earnest voice. "I don't understand why those women want to come to the West and try to change things."

"They very much believe in what they are doing," Longarm explained. "They are just asking for the right to vote, and they oppose liquor as if it were a poison."

"I have no problem with giving 'em the right to vote, Marshal. But prohibition? What in the world for? Things are tough enough out here without taking away a Western man's precious few pleasures. Some people use religion as their way to put up with a bad life, some use alcohol. It can work either way to make things bearable."

"I happen to agree with you that we ought to be able to drink, Maynard," Longarm said, noticing the man's name stenciled on his Western Union employee's badge. "But I also believe that both of those suffragists have a Constitutional right to voice their opinions."

"What about using a hatchet to bust up saloons?"

"That's where their rights end and the rights of the saloon owner begin."

"But you didn't arrest the woman," Maynard said, his voice faintly accusing.

"No, I didn't. It seemed a far better idea to send her packing."

"Yeah, I guess it was."

They chatted for a half hour or more until Longarm's return telegram came over the wire. It was short, and not particularly sweet.

> CUT YOUR LOSSES AND OUR DEPARTMENT'S EXPENSES **STOP** RETURN EASTWARD AS FAR AS POSSIBLE WITH MISS BELCHER **STOP** WE MAY YET SALVAGE OUR CAREERS **STOP**

Maynard handed Longarm the telegraph, saying, "It doesn't sound too good, does it, Marshal."

"No," Longarm conceded, "it does not. However, I can't leave Miss Howe, no matter how slim the odds are that someone still considers her a threat or an easy target. So send back my reply to read:

> 'I'M STAYING FOR REASONS ALREADY STATED **STOP** OUR FEDERAL CAREERS BE DAMNED **STOP**'..."

Maynard liked that. He even forgot how worried he was and chuckled until Longarm said, "Watch your backside for the next few hours, just in case."

The telegraph operator's grin faded like ice on a hot skillet. "Marshal, are you serious?"

"When it comes to trapping a murderer, I'm *always* serious," Longarm said on his way out the door, thinking that he might go pay Miss Howe a visit.

• • •

Katherine Howe was still bedridden from her bullet wound, but feeling much stronger. When she had become strong enough, she'd taken up residence at the house of Mrs. Georgia Billings, a woman widowed by a well-respected doctor who had caught pneumonia the previous winter and quickly passed away. Mrs. Billings was an excellent nurse and caretaker, and so was well suited to assist in Katherine's recovery. She had taken an immediate liking to the willowy Eastern girl, and being somewhat of a romantic and a lover of poetry, had also befriended young Steven Fishburn.

"I think she takes better care of you than she does me," Katherine was saying with amusement as she and Steven enjoyed their second cup of morning tea.

From Katherine's room, Steven watched Mrs. Billings leave the house, turn at her front gate, and leave to do her morning shopping. "She is a wonderful lady. I appreciate the fact that she trusts me to remain here unattended with you."

"Mrs. Billings knows that you are a gentleman."

Steven moved his chair a little closer. He leaned forward and took Katherine's hand. "Even though I write poetry, words escape me completely when I attempt to say how much I love you. And that you have agreed to marry me seems like a dream come true."

"I'm the one that has found my dream come true," Katherine told him. "I knew when you jumped up on that stage with bullets flying in every direction, and then shielded me with your own body, that you were my prince in shining armor. My hero."

Steven blushed. "I love you, Katherine, but I am concerned for your safety."

"I won't do any more public speaking. At least, not about prohibition. But concerning women having the right to vote, I simply can't be silent. It's too unfair."

"I agree. But when you begin to speak about outlawing liquor, well, men become irrational."

"Drunks are *always* irrational."

"I know," Steven said. "My father has long been a slave to whiskey. When he becomes drunk, he is possessed by inner demons too terrible to imagine. That's why I don't touch liquor."

"You're afraid of it."

"I am."

Steven was about to elaborate when he heard footsteps in the hallway. "Who is that? Mrs. Billings?"

"She must have returned for something forgotten," Katherine said, eyes turning toward the open door.

But it *wasn't* Mrs. Billings who filled the doorway. Instead, it was a large, very wide man with a very big Bowie knife in his fist.

"Steven!"

Steven felt his blood turn to ice. He jumped up from his chair and placed himself between the big man and Katherine. Somehow, he managed to say, "If you've come to rob this house, then do so but leave us alone!"

"I'll loot it, all right. Dr. Billings made a lot of money and I know that there's some precious things to be taken." The man advanced a couple of steps into the room and smiled thinly. "But I can't very well leave witnesses, can I?"

"Please, we have nothing of value!" Steven exclaimed.

But the intruder took another step forward. "When I go, I'll leave the signs of a thief who took what he wanted and then set this house on fire. Neat, huh?"

Katherine inhaled deeply. Her derringer was in her purse, and her purse was on the dresser just out of reach.

"Who *are* you?" Steven asked.

"Just a man who is about to do the job that he was paid to do," the man answered.

"Then you're not just here by chance?"

"Naw! Miss Belcher is gone, but your little lady love is still around."

"Who hired you?"

The intruder beamed as if that amused him. "Mr. Fishburn, that's for me to know and you to wonder about as you depart this cruel world."

Katherine eased closer to the dresser and her purse. "Please don't hurt us! I have a little money!"

"Sure you do," the man said with his thin smile. "And I'll take that. Been watchin' Mrs. Billings the last two days, and she won't be back until almost noon. Course by then, this house will be nothin' but a pile of smokin' ashes. The volunteer fire companies up here are damned slow."

Katherine was so scared that she could hardly breathe. Steven was standing in front of her, but she could see the intruder's face and she knew that he was about to jump forward and cut both their throats. He was so powerful that Steven wouldn't stand a chance. It was now . . . or never.

"I'll show you how much money I have in my purse," she said without looking at the killer anymore because if she did, she would certainly lose her nerve.

The killer hesitated just a moment, and that was long enough for Katherine to make a lunge for her purse, almost throwing herself out of bed. "Look!" she cried as her fist closed around the handle of her derringer.

The killer attacked at the very same instant that Steven grabbed her pillow and hurled it into his face. While the man was momentarily blinded, Katherine fired. Her shot went through the pillow and struck the man in the right side of his jaw. Feathers flew up in a cloud as the slug plowed through his mouth to exit from his opposite cheek. Both she and Steven heard his muffled scream as his knees buckled. The attacker struck the floor at the foot of the bed and tried to rise. He would have too, except that Steven grabbed the water pitcher, raised it high, and then smashed the man over the head, shattering the porcelain to bits.

"Get his knife!" Katherine shouted.

Steven tore it out of their attacker's hands, and his mind was in such a fever that he slashed the big man across the back of his thick neck. Fortunately, the wound was not deep, or it might have severed the spinal cord. However, more blood poured from the man's neck to join that from his shattered jaw. When the dazed assailant saw all the gore, he fainted.

"Tie him up!"

"Katherine, he's bleeding to death!"

"I don't care! Tie him up and *then* we'll see if we can save his miserable life!"

Steven tore off his suspenders and managed to tie the assailant's hands behind his back. He looked up at Katherine, saying, "Honey, you were absolutely magnificent! You saved both our lives."

"You helped. After we're married, I'm going to teach you how to shoot a gun whether you want to or not."

"I *want to,* darling!"

It was right about then that Longarm dashed into the house. He'd heard the shot and the shouting. When he skidded to a halt and surveyed the carnage, he could hardly believe his eyes.

"Who is this man!"

"He's not just a thief," Steven replied. "He came to kill Miss Howe and admitted that he was *paid* by someone."

Longarm dropped to one knee beside the fallen attacker. The man was bleeding fast, and it was doubtful that he would survive unless he received a doctor's immediate attention. However, he was the key that would open the door to whoever was behind this entire assassination conspiracy.

"Who hired you?" Longarm shouted, grabbing the man by the back of his hair and twisting his head around.

"He can't speak!" Steven cried. "Marshal, can't you see that his jaw is shattered?"

It was true. The man was losing consciousness and his mouth was hanging open.

"All right," Longarm said. "Steven, go find a doctor and get him here fast. We've got to save this vermin until he can either talk or write."

Steven shot out of the room, and returned in minutes. "We're in luck," he cried. "The doctor was coming to see Katherine and he's right behind me!"

Longarm was getting more hopeful by the moment. The facial wound, while terrible, was certainly not fatal. There was a huge lump rising on the man's forehead where he'd been struck by the shattered water pitcher, and a superficial slash wound across his neck, but none of them added up to enough to kill a bruiser like this.

"You're going to tell me who hired you," Longarm growled at the unconscious man. "This time, there will be no back-alley bullet to silence the truth! By gawd, this time I'll find out who is behind this if I have to make you write their names in your own blood!"

Chapter 16

The doctor came out of the room and spoke to Longarm. "Marshal, your prisoner will probably survive, but it will be impossible for him to speak for a long, long time, if ever. His tongue was badly wounded, and both sides of his jawbone were shattered by the bullet that Miss Howe fired. It is a miracle that he is even alive considering how much blood he lost and then swallowed."

"I've *got* to find out who hired him to kill Miss Howe. Is he awake?"

"Yes, but I've given him some opium to counter the intense pain and he is groggy."

"Can he understand what is going on?"

"I expect so."

Longarm stepped around the doctor, who tried to block his entrance, saying, "Marshal, my patient is in terrible pain! He's also swallowed a lot of his own blood and his lungs are half filled with it. He may not yet survive. I can't have you in there badgering him!''

Longarm removed the doctor's hand from his arm. ''Doc,'' he said, ''I've *got* to find out who hired him before there is another attempt on Miss Howe's life. Furthermore, I expect that someone might even attempt to kill this man in order to protect themselves.''

The doctor sighed with resignation. ''I see. Very well, then. You can see him, but he still won't be able to speak.''

''I'll just have to hope that he can write down the name of whoever hired him. Do you have a paper and pencil?''

''Of course.''

''I only want a few private minutes with the man,'' Longarm said.

''Very well,'' the doctor agreed.

After the doctor provided Longarm with writing materials, the lawman went into the surgery room and stood by his prisoner for a moment, studying his ruined and now heavily bandaged face. Sensing his presence, the hired gunman opened his eyes and glared at Longarm with the most hateful expression imaginable.

''You can understand me, right?''

The man made no attempt to respond, so Longarm drew his six-gun and placed the barrel of it under the man's shattered jaw, saying, ''I could put another bullet through your cheek and jaw.''

The prisoner's eyes widened, but he made no attempt to communicate, so Longarm added, ''I'll put it to you this way. You can write down the name of whoever hired you to kill Miss Howe, or you'll suffer even more."

When the man snorted through his nose with derision, Longarm tapped his shattered jaw hard with his gun barrel. The prisoner would have screamed in pain if Longarm hadn't clamped his hand over his mouth.

"I want the name of whoever paid you to kill Miss Howe or I'll toss you out of here. You won't last an hour out on the street because whoever hired you will kill you to keep you silent. Now, what is it going to be?"

The prisoner motioned for the pencil and paper.

"You are going to prison for attempted murder. But since you failed, you'll be out in a couple of years, and that's by far your best and only deal. Understand?"

The prisoner nodded. Longarm gave the man the writing materials, and he wrote:

HIRAM DAWSON PAID ME.

"Doctor!"

"Yes, Marshal?" said the doctor, coming into the room.

"Who is Hiram Dawson?"

"He owns the Truckee Wagon Company."

"What do they haul?"

"Everything except ore. It's the biggest supply freighter on the Comstock Lode."

"Do you suppose they haul liquor?"

"Sure!"

Longarm returned his attention to the wounded prisoner. "If you attempt to escape or harm this doctor, I'll swear that I'll shoot you on sight. Is that understood?''

The big man made it clear he understood.

''If you've lied to me, I'll feed you to whoever *really* paid you to kill Miss Howe. Is that also understood?''

Again, the man indicated that, opium notwithstanding, he comprehended.

Longarm turned back to the doctor. ''Where is the Truckee Wagon Company?''

''They've got a stockyard and office down on the corner of Taylor and D Street. It's right across from St. Mary of the Mountains Catholic Church.''

''That's where I'm heading,'' Longarm said. ''What does Mr. Dawson look like?''

''He's a tall, thin fella with a full beard shot with gray. He moves with a limp he said he got fighting in the Civil War, and uses a stout hickory cane. He has a fearsome temper, and I've seen him whip both his men and his animals. He's a hotheaded and ill-tempered man.''

Longarm turned back to his prisoner, who was listening closely. ''Does Dawson carry a hideout weapon?''

The prisoner nodded.

''Did Dawson hire the man who opened fire at Piper's Opera House killing the deputy and wounding Miss Howe?''

Again, the prisoner nodded.

''Okay, then,'' Longarm said, wagging the paper that his prisoner had used to save his own hide. ''I'll arrest Hiram Dawson for conspiracy and the murder of Reno Deputy Doug Potter as well as for the attempted murder of both Miss Belcher and Miss Howe. That ought to be enough to put him away for the rest of his natural life.''

''Marshal?''

“Yes?”

The doctor looked very worried. “You'd better take some help. Hiram Dawson isn't going to submit to being arrested, and you're going to be surrounded by his employees. They're a rough bunch, and despite their hard treatment, I expect that Dawson pays them well and they are loyal.”

“I can handle them,” Longarm replied as he went out the door.

In front of the Silver Dollar, he ran into Dan De Quille, and the newspaperman rushed up to him and said, “Custis, what can you tell me about this second attempt on Miss Howe's life?”

“I've got the attacker under arrest and he admits to being hired by Hiram Dawson, owner of the Truckee Wagon Company. I'm on my way to arrest the man.”

“Alone?”

“That's right.”

“Please,” the newspaperman begged, “wait just a minute while I step into this saloon.”

“Dan, if you need a drink that badly. . . .”

“It could save your life, Marshal!”

Something told Longarm to give his friend a few moments, though he had no idea of De Quille's intentions. In a few moments, however, they were made clear when Dan burst back outside with no less than ten armed miners in his wake.

“Custis, mark my word—you're going to need some folks to back you up,” Dan told him, a gun clenched in one bony hand and a pencil and pad in the other. “Trust me, it will make things *much* easier.”

Longarm did trust the star reporter of the *Territorial*

Enterprise, and decided not to object when Dan and his friends followed him down C Street. They made an abrupt left turn onto Taylor Street, and marched down the steep hillside to enter the wagon yard. It was a hub of activity, with at least a dozen supply wagons being loaded or unloaded. Men were shouting and mules were braying and fidgeting in their harness. At the sight of so many armed men following Longarm, the freight company employees froze and stared.

"What's going on?" the one who seemed to be in charge of the yard demanded.

"I'm Marshal—"

"I know who the hell you are! What do you want?"

"I want to see Mr. Dawson."

The man folded his muscular arms across his chest and said smugly, "Sorry, but Mr. Dawson ain't here today."

"You'd better not be lying," Longarm warned, "or I'll haul your ass down to Carson City and have you face a judge for obstruction of justice!"

The man's smugness evaporated. "The boss might be inside after all, Marshal."

Longarm stomped into the freight office, surprising three employees in white shirts and black ties. "Where's Mr. Dawson!"

"My name is Jacobson," a short heavyset man in a baggy suit announced. "What right do you have to interrupt our business?"

"I'm here to arrest Hiram Dawson for murder and conspiracy to murder."

"You are out of your gawdamn mind!"

Longarm ripped a short but brutal uppercut that collided with the point of the man's underslung jaw. His eyes crossed, and he dropped like an anvil. When he tried to get up, Longarm stomped a boot heel down on his fat belly and shouted, "You got one chance to tell me where Hiram Dawson went! Don't lie to me and put yourself into any worse of a mess than you already are!"

Jacobson was gasping like a beached whale. Longarm watched as the man rolled his head sideways and point with his finger toward a closed door.

"Dawson! Come out or I'm coming in after you!" Longarm shouted, drawing his side arm.

There was no answer. Longarm went to the door and tried to turn the knob, but it was locked.

"Marshal! He went out the back window!" one of the armed miners shouted from out in the freight yard.

Longarm whirled and sprinted back outside. He raced around the large building, and saw a man laboring toward the Virginia & Truckee Railroad Depot. He knew that it was Hiram Dawson because the man carried a cane and was limping badly.

"Dawson!"

Longarm's shout was immediately followed by the ear-piercing sound of a locomotive steam whistle. Longarm realized that the freight company owner was trying desperately to reach the train as it began to ease out of the V&T depot on its way down to Carson City.

"Stop!" Longarm cried.

But Dawson had no intention of stopping. In addition to his cane, he was lugging a black satchel, and Longarm was willing to bet his own meager bank account that the satchel was stuffed with money.

"Stop!"

As Dawson neared the departing train, Longarm decided that he was not going to be able to prevent him from getting on board. That meant that he either shot and killed Dawson right now, or else tried to overtake the train and make an arrest. Then he could determine if Dawson was working alone or not.

Longarm decided to try to take his man alive and get a full confession. Nothing less would save his and Billy Vail's jobs back in Denver. The decision made, he lowered his head and ran as hard as he could as the train gathered speed. His lungs were burning and his feet were flying. He had powerful legs, but Virginia City rested at well over six thousand feet and the air was thin.

Once, Longarm almost fell and took a tumble across the cinders of the railroad tracks, but he managed to regain his balance and keep upright. With the very last of his failing strength, he overtook the caboose and catapulted on board. Longarm collapsed to his knees, fighting for breath to put out the fire in his burning lungs.

He was still bent over and gasping when the rear door of the caboose swung wide open and Dawson attacked him with his hickory cane. Longarm threw up his left arm, and felt it go numb as he deflected a whistling blow that would have cracked his skull like an eggshell. He took a second blow across his left shoulder that momentarily paralyzed that entire side down to his waist. Then, unwilling to suffer another blow, he managed to put a bullet through Dawson's foot.

"Ahhhh!" the man screamed, flailing at Longarm while hopping about on one foot.

Longarm took a glancing blow over his ear that made

his vision blur. Afraid that he might yet be bludgeoned to death, Longarm began firing again.

When Longarm's vision cleared, Dawson was lying beside him with three more slugs in his legs that ranged from his ankle to his crotch. Longarm grabbed him by the throat. "I've got two more bullets to spare, and I'll put the next one into your gawdamn brain if you don't tell me who else was behind the conspiracy to assassinate Miss Belcher and Miss Howe!"

"I don't know what you're talking about!" the man sobbed.

"You're lying!"

"I'm bleeding to death! Help me!"

Longarm was in considerable pain himself. His left arm and shoulder were still numb, and he felt sick to his stomach and was very close to passing out. Even so, he dragged the bloodstained paper out of his pocket with the penciled words "HIRAM DAWSON PAID ME."

"I've got your hired killer in custody and you're headed for the gallows!"

Dawson stared up at him with crazy, rolling eyes. Then, his hand stabbed into his pocket and before Longarm could react, the man shot himself to death with his own hideout gun.

Two weeks later, Steven and Katherine were married before a small but happy group of Comstock Lode friends, including Steven's best man, Marshal Custis Long.

"We're going to stay here in Virginia City," Steven told him. "I've been commissioned to do some important paintings. Mr. De Quille and I are also talking about writing a lively history of Comstock Lode and sending it to Mark Twain to see if he can help us get it published and distributed out of New York City.''

''I wish you both all the best,'' Longarm said with deepest sincerity.

''Custis, when are you returning to Denver?'' Katherine asked as they strolled down C Street to enjoy a small but lavish reception.

''I'm leaving tomorrow,'' Longarm answered, adjusting the sling that supported his broken left shoulder. ''I've been exchanging telegrams with my boss, who assures me that *his* bosses are quite pleased with the outcome of our . . . Comstock adventure.''

Mrs. Katherine Fishburn, radiant in her wedding gown, kissed Longarm's cheek, and then Steven pumped his hand, saying, ''I can't believe all that has happened just since I met you on the stagecoach coming up here less than two months ago.''

Somehow, Longarm managed a smile. ''Neither can I,'' he assured the young groom. ''Neither can I.''

Watch for

LONGARM AND THE BLOSSOM ROCK BANSHEE

238th novel in the exciting LONGARM series from Jove

Coming in October!